*Harun smiled—n*___ *made you think I* ___ *~~wishy-wasny~~* Yes, dear, of course dear *kind of wife?"*

In all this time I've never seen him smile like that.

Right now, kidnapped and in this strange place, he was all she had—just as she was all he had—and the thought of losing this smiling man, now teasing her and caressing her hand, was unbearable.

"Well, maybe if you'd talked to me about what kind of wife you did want, I could answer that," she replied, in a light, fun tone. "But right now I'm rather clueless."

At that, he chuckled. "Yes, you're not the only one who's told me that I keep a little too much to myself."

Fascinated, she stared at his mouth. "In all this time, I've never heard you laugh."

She half expected him to make a cool retort—but instead, one end of his mouth quirked higher. "You think it took being abducted for me to show my true colors? Maybe, if you like it, we can arrange for it to happen on a regular basis?"

MELISSA JAMES

The Sheikh's Jewel

TORONTO NEW YORK LONDON
AMSTERDAM PARIS SYDNEY HAMBURG
STOCKHOLM ATHENS TOKYO MILAN MADRID
PRAGUE WARSAW BUDAPEST AUCKLAND

Recycling programs
for this product may
not exist in your area.

ISBN-13: 978-0-373-17816-2

THE SHEIKH'S JEWEL

First North American Publication 2012

Copyright © 2012 by Lisa Chaplin

Melissa James is a born-and-bred Sydneysider. Wife and mother of three, and a former nurse, she fell into writing when her husband brought home an article about romance writers and suggested she try it—and she became hooked. Switching from romantic espionage to the family stories of the Harlequin Romance® line was the best move she ever made.

Melissa loves to hear from readers—you can email her at authormelissajames@yahoo.com.

Books by Melissa James

ONE SMALL MIRACLE
THE SHEIKH'S DESTINY

Other titles by this author available in ebook format.

To my editor, Bryony Green, with my deepest thanks for all her help as I tried to make the deadline for this book during an international move

CHAPTER ONE

Sar Abbas, capital city of Abbas al-Din
Three years ago

'Is this a joke?'

Sitting straight-backed in an overstuffed chair, her body swathed in the black of deep mourning, Amber el-Qurib stared up at her father in disbelief. 'Please, Father, tell me you're trying to make me laugh.' But even as she pleaded she knew it was hopeless.

Her father, Sheikh Aziz of Araba Numara—Land of the Tiger—was also wearing mourning clothes, but his face was composed. He'd wept enough the first day, in the same shock as everyone else; but he hadn't cried since, apart from a few decorous tears at Fadi's funeral. 'Do you think I would make jokes about your future, Amber, or play with a decision that is so important to our nation?' His tone bordered on withering.

Yes, she ought to have known. Though he'd been a kind father, in all her life, she'd never heard her father make a joke about anything relating to the welfare of Araba Numara.

'My fiancé only died six weeks ago.' Amber forced the words out through a throat thick with weeks of tears. He'd been the co-driver for his younger brother Alim, in just one rally. The Double Racing Sheikhs had caused a great deal of mirth and media interest in Abbas al-Din, as had the upcoming wedding.

Even now it seemed surreal. How could Fadi be *dead*—and how could she marry his brother within another month, as her father wanted? How could it even be done while Alim was fighting for his life, with second- and third-degree burns? 'It—it isn't decent,' she said, trying to sound strong but, as ever when with her father, she floundered under the weight of her own opinion. Was she right?

And when her father sighed, giving her the long-suffering look she'd always hated—it made her feel selfish, or like a silly girl—she knew she'd missed something, as usual. 'There are some things more important than how we appear to others. You understand how it is, Amber.'

She did. Both their countries had fallen into uproar after Sheikh Fadi's sudden death in a car wreck. The beloved leader of Abbas al-Din had been lost before he could marry and father a legitimate son, and Amber's people had lost a union that was expected to bring closer ties to a nation far stronger and wealthier than theirs.

It was vital at this point that both nations find stability. The people needed hope: for Araba Numara, that they'd have that permanent connection to Abbas al-Din, and Fadi's people needed to know the el-Kanar family line would continue.

She swiped at her eyes again. Damn Fadi! He'd risked his life a week before their wedding, knowing he didn't want her and she didn't want him—but thousands of marriages had started with less than the respect and liking they'd had for one another. They could have worked it out—but now the whispers were circulating.

She'd endured some impertinent insinuations, from the maids to Ministers of State. That much she could bear, if only she didn't have doubts of her own, deep-held fears that woke her every night.

She'd known he wasn't happy—was deeply unhappy—at the arranged marriage; but *had* Fadi risked death to avoid marrying her?

Certainly neither of them had been in love, but that wasn't uncommon. Fadi had been deeply in love with his mistress, the sweet widow who'd borne his son. But with probably the only impulsive decision he'd ever made, he'd left his country leaderless in a minute. At the moment Alim, his brother and the remaining heir, was still fighting for his life.

'Amber?' her father asked, his tone caught between exasperation and uncertainty. 'The dynasty here must continue, and very quickly. We only gain from the mother of the dynasty being one of our daughters.'

'Then let it continue with someone else! Haven't I done enough?'

'Who do you suggest? Maya is not yet seventeen. Nafisah is but fourteen, and Amal twelve. Your cousins are of similar age to them.' Her father made a savage noise. 'You are the eldest, already here, and bound to the el-Kanar family. They are obligated by their ancient law on brides to care for you, and find you a husband within the family line. Everything—tradition, law, honour and the good of your family—demands that you accept this offer.'

Shamed but still furious, Amber kept her mouth tightly closed. Why must all this fall on her shoulders? She wanted to cry out, *I'm only nineteen!*

Why did some get responsibilities in life, and others all the fun? Alim had shrugged off his responsibilities to the nation for years, chasing fame and wealth on the racing circuit while Fadi and the youngest brother— what was his name again?—had done all the work. Yes, Alim was famous around the world, and had brought so much wealth to the nation with his career in geological surveys and excavation.

And then she realised what—or *who* it was she could be turning down. Even though a sudden marriage repulsed her sense of what felt right in her grief for the man she'd cared for deeply as a friend, the thought of *who* she must be marrying didn't repulse her at all.

Her father laid a hand on her shoulder. It was only with the long years of training that she managed not to shrug off the rare gesture of affection, knowing it was only given to make her stop arguing. For women of her status, any emotion was a luxury one only indulged in among the safety of other women, or not at all if one had the necessary pride. 'You know how it is, Amber. We *need* this marriage. One brother or another, what does it matter to you? You barely knew Fadi before your engagement was agreed upon. You only came to stay here two months before he died, and most of the time he was working or gone.'

Blushing, Amber turned her head, looking at the ground to the left of her feet. *Such a beautiful rug,* she thought inconsequentially; but no matter what she looked at, it didn't block out the memory of where Fadi had gone whenever he had spare time—to his mistress. And always he'd come back with Rafa's smell on his skin, some mumbled apologies and yet another promise he'd never see Rafa again when they were married: a promise given with heartbreak in his eyes.

Amber felt the shadows of the past envelop her. She alone knew where the fault lay with Fadi's death. Sweet, kind, gentle Fadi had always done the right thing, including agreeing to marry another ruler's daughter for political gain, when he was deeply in love with an unsuitable commoner, a former housemaid...and Amber, too, had feelings for another, if only from afar. And nobody knew it but the three people whose lives were being torn apart.

She knew Fadi would never wish her harm, but if it had been Amber who'd died suddenly, it would have set him free to be with Rafa—at least for a little while, until the next arranged political marriage.

She truly grieved for the loss of the gentle-hearted ruler, as she would grieve for any friend lost. Fadi had understood her feelings and sympathised with her, was like the moon's sweet light in her darkness. So—was it awful of her to feel this sudden little thrill that her wayward heart's feelings were no longer forbidden?

Fadi, I did care for you. I'm so sorry, but you're the only one who'd understand...

'I'm still in deep mourning, and you expect me to marry his brother while he's still in hospital with second- and third-degree burns? Won't that look—well, rather desperate on our part?' she mumbled, wishing she had something better to say, wishing she didn't feel quite so excited. Hoping to heaven her father wouldn't see it on her face. 'Can't you ask Alim if he'd be willing to wait a few months for the wedding—?'

'You will not be marrying Alim,' her father interrupted her bluntly.

Amber's head shot up. *'What?'*

'I'm sorry, my dear,' her father said quietly. 'Alim disappeared from the hospital last night, unequivocally refusing both Fadi's position and Fadi's bride. I doubt he'll return for a long time, if ever.'

Amber almost snarled—almost. Women of her station didn't snarl, not even when the man she—she *liked* had just run out on her; but she managed to hang onto her self-control. 'Where did he go? How did he manage it?'

'Within hours of waking, Alim used his private jet and his medical team from the racing circuit to help him transfer to a private facility—we think he went somewhere in Switzerland. He still needs a lot of graft work on his burns, but he made it obvious that he won't return here when it's done.'

'He must have been desperate to escape from me, leaving hospital when he's at death's door,' she muttered, fighting off a sudden jolt of queasiness in her stomach.

'I doubt it was a personal rejection, my dear. He hardly knew you. I think it was perhaps more of—ah, a matter of principle, or a reaction made in grief.' Her father slanted her a look of semi-apology; so he was capable of embarrassment, at least. 'I find it hard to blame him, after the part he played in Fadi's death… imagine him waking up to find Fadi's skin on his body. He must have felt he'd taken enough from his brother— life, skin…it must be horrifying enough, but wedding and bedding Fadi's bride on top of all that must have felt as if he'd done it all on purpose.'

'Indeed,' she agreed, but with a trace of bitterness. Surely this day couldn't get any worse?

'Since you won't ask, I'll tell you. The youngest brother Harun has taken up the position as Hereditary Sheikh, and has agreed also to become your husband.'

The swirling winds of change had come right from the sun, scorching her to her core. 'Of course he has!' Amber didn't know she spoke aloud, the fury of rejection boiling over. 'So having been rejected by brothers one and two, I'm expected to—to wed and bed brother number three with a smile? There are limits to the amount of humiliation I must accept, surely, Father?'

'You will accept whatever I arrange for you, Amber.' His voice now was pure ice. 'And you should be grateful that I have given such thought to your marriage.'

'Oh, such thought indeed, Father! Why not send me to the princess pound? Because that's what I've become to you, isn't it—a dog, a piece of property returned for you to find a good home and husband elsewhere? Find another owner for Amber because *we* don't want her back.'

'Stop it,' her father said sharply. 'You're a beautiful woman. Many men have wanted to marry you, but I chose the el-Kanar brothers because they are truly good men.'

'Oh, yes, I know that well,' she mocked, knowing Father would punish her for this unprecedented outburst later, but not caring. 'Unfortunately for me, it seems they're good men who'd do anything to avoid me.' She spoke as coldly as she could—anything to hide the tears stinging her eyes and the huge lump in her throat. Alim, the wild and dashing Racing Sheikh, had risked his recovery, his very life to get away from her. As far as insults went, it outranked Fadi's by a million miles. 'Am I so repulsive, Father? What's wrong with me?'

'I see you are in need of relieving your, ah, feelings,' her father said with a strong streak of cold disapproval that she had *feelings* to vent. 'But we are not home, Amber. Royal women do not scream or make emotional outbursts.'

'I can't believe the last remaining brother in the dynasty is willing to risk it,' she pushed in the stinging acid of grief and humiliation without relief. 'Perhaps you should offer him one of my sisters instead, because it seems the el-Kanar men are allergic to me.'

'The Lord Harun has expressed complete willingness to marry you, Amber,' her father said in quiet rebuke.

'Oh, how noble is Brother Number Three, to take the unwanted responsibilities of his older brothers, nation and wife alike, when the other just can't face it!'

'Amber,' her father said sharply. 'That's enough. Your future husband has a name. You will not shame him, or our family, in this manner. He's lost enough!'

She knew what was expected of her. 'I'm sorry, Father. I will behave,' she said dully. She dragged a breath in and out, willing calm, some form of decorum. 'That was uncalled for. I have nothing against the Lord—um, Harun, and I apologise, Father.'

'You should apologise.' Her father's voice was cold with disapproval. 'Harun was only eight when his father died in the plane crash, and his mother died three months later. For the past six weeks he's been grieving for a brother who had been more like a father to him, and he couldn't stop working long enough to stay at the hospital while the only brother he has left, his only close living relative, was fighting for his life. With so many high-ranking families wanting to take over the sudden wealth in Abbas al-Din, Harun had to assume the sheikh's position and run the country in Alim's name, not knowing if Alim would live or die. Now Harun's been left completely alone with the responsibility of running the nation and marrying you, and all this while he's in deepest mourning. He's lost his entire family. Is it so much to ask that you could stop mocking him, be a woman and help him in his time of greatest need?'

Amber felt the flush of shame cover her face.

Whatever she'd lost, Harun had by far the worst suffering of them all. 'No, it isn't. I'm truly sorry, Father. It's just that—well, he's so quiet,' she tried to explain, feeling the inadequacy of her words. 'He never says anything to me apart from good morning or goodnight. He barely even looks at me. He's a stranger, a complete stranger, and now I must marry him in a month's time? Can't we have a little time to know each other first— just a few months?'

'It must be now,' her father said, his voice sad, and she searched his face. He had a way of making her feel guilty without trying, but this time he seemed sincere. 'The sharks are circling Harun—you know how unstable the entire Gulf region has been the past two years. The el-Shabbat family ruled hundreds of years ago, until Muran's madness led to the coup that gave power to Aswan, the greatest of the el-Kanar clan, two hundred and fifty years ago. The el-Shabbat leaders believe the el-Kanar clan are interlopers, and if they ever had a chance to take control of the army and kill the remaining family members, it is now.'

Amber's hand lifted to her mouth. Lost in her own fog of grief, she'd had no idea things were so bad. 'They will kill Lord Harun?'

He nodded. 'And Alim, too, while he's still so weak. It's a good thing nobody knows exactly where he went. All it would take is one corrupt doctor or nurse and a dose of poison into his IV bag, and the el-Shabbats will rule Abbas al-Din once more—a nation with far greater wealth and stability than they ever knew while they were in power.'

'I see,' she said quietly.

'And we need this alliance, my dear daughter. You were but one of twenty well-born girls offered to Fadi—

and to Harun—in the past few years. We are the far poorer, less stable nation, and yet they chose alliance with our family and nation. It's a blessing to our nation I hardly expected; it's given our people hope. And I must say, in my dealings with all three brothers, Harun is the man I'd have chosen for you if I'd had the choice.'

His voice softened on the last sentence, but Amber barely noticed. 'So the contract has been signed,' she said dully. 'I have no choice in this at all.' Her only decision was to go down fighting, or accept her future with grace.

'No, my dear, you don't.' The words were gentle, but inflexible. 'It has been inevitable from the moment the Lord Harun was made aware of his duty towards you.'

She pressed her lips together hard, fighting unseemly tears. Perhaps she should be grateful that the Lord Harun wasn't leaving her to face her public shame— but another man willing to marry her from duty alone left her stomach churning. At least she'd known and liked Fadi. 'But he doesn't even look at me. He never talks to me. I never know what he's thinking or feeling about anything.' *Including me.* 'How am I to face this—this total stranger in the marriage bed, Father? Can you answer me that?'

'It's what many women have done for thousands of years, including your mother and my grandmother Kahlidah, the nation's heroine you've always admired so much. She was only seventeen when she wed my grandfather—another stranger—and within a year, eighteen, pregnant and a new widow, she stopped the invasion of Araba Numara, ruling the nation with strength and wisdom until my father was old enough to take over. Do as she had to, and grow a backbone, child! What is your fear for one night, compared to what Harun faces, and alone?' her father shot back.

Never had her father spoken to her with such contempt and coldness. She drew another breath and released it as she willed strength into her heart. 'I'll do my duty, of course, Father, and do my best to support Lord Harun in all he faces. Perhaps we can find mutual friendship in our loss and our need.'

Father smiled at her, and patted her hand. 'That's more like my strong Amber. Harun is a truly good man, for all his quiet ways. I know—' he clearly hesitated, and Amber writhed inside, waiting for what she'd give anything for him *not* to say '—I know you…admired Lord Alim. What young woman wouldn't admire the Racing Sheikh, with his dashing ways, his wins on the racing circuit worldwide, and the power and wealth he's brought to this region?'

'Please stop,' she murmured in anguish. 'Please, Father, no more.'

But he went on remorselessly. 'Amber, my child, you are so young—too young to understand that the men who change history are not always the Alexanders, or even the Alims,' he added, with a strained smile. 'The real heroes are usually unsung, making their contributions in silence. I believe Lord Harun is one of them. My advice is for you to look at the man I've chosen for you, and ask yourself why I brought this offer to him, not even wanting to wait for Alim's recovery. I think that, if you give Harun a chance, you'll find you and he are very well suited. You can have a good life together, if you will put your heart and soul behind your vows.'

'Yes, Father,' Amber said, feeling dull and spiritless at the thought of being *well suited* and having *a good life,* when she'd had a moment's dream of marrying the man she—well, she thought she could have loved, given time…

At that moment, a movement behind the door caught her eye. *Damn* the officious staffers and inquisitive servants, always listening in, looking for more gossip to spread far and wide! She lifted her chin and sent her most icy stare to the unknown entity at the door. She felt the presence move back a step, and another.

Good. She hoped they'd run far away. If she must deal with these intrusive servants, they'd best know the calibre of the woman who was to be their future mistress—and mistress she'd be.

'If you wouldn't mind, Father, I'd like to—to have a little time alone,' she said quietly.

'You still grieve for Fadi. You're a good girl.' Her father patted her hand, and left the room by the private exit between their rooms.

The moment the connecting door closed, Amber said coldly, 'If I discover any of you are listening in or I hear gossip repeated about this conversation, I will ensure the lot of you are dismissed without a reference. Is that clear?'

It was only when she heard the soft shuffling of feet moving away that Amber at last fell to her bed and cried. Cried again for the loss of a gentle-hearted friend, cried for the end of an unspoken dream—and she cried for the nightmare facing her.

Frozen two steps back from the partially open door to the rooms of state allotted to the Princess Amber, the man who was the subject of his guests' recent discussion had long since dropped the hand he'd held up to knock. Harun el-Kanar's upbringing hadn't included eavesdropping on intimate conversations—and had he not frozen in horror, he wouldn't have heard Amber so desperately trying to get out of marrying him. He wouldn't have seen that repellent look, like a shard of ice piercing his skin.

So now he knew his future wife's opinion of him… and it was little short of pure revulsion. Why did it even surprise him?

Turning sharply away, he strode towards the sanctuary of his rooms. He needed peace, a few minutes to think—

'Lord Harun, there is a call from the Prince al-Hassan of Saudi regarding the deal with Emirates Oil. He is most anxious to speak with you about the Lord Alim's recent find of oil.'

'Of course, I will come now,' he answered quietly, and walked with his personal assistant back to his office.

When the call was done, his minister of state came in. 'My Lord, in the absence of the Lord Alim, we need your immediate presence in the House for a swearing-in ceremony. For the stability of the country, this must be done as soon as possible. I know you will understand the anxiety of your people to have this reassurance that you are committed to the ongoing welfare of Abbas al-Din.'

His assistant raced in with his robes of state, helping Harun into them before he could make a reply.

During the next five hours, as he sat and stood and bowed and made a speech of acceptance of his new role, none of those hereditary leaders sensed how deeply their new sheikh grieved for a brother nine years older. Fadi had been more like a father to him.

Could any of them see how utterly alone he was now, since Alim's disappearance? He hid it behind the face of years of training, calm and regal. They needed the perfect sheikh, and they'd have one for as long as it was needed. Members of the ruling family were trained almost from birth—they must display no need beyond the privilege of serving their people. But during the ceremony, in moments when he didn't have complete control of his mind, Harun had unbidden visions: of eyes as warm as melted honey, and skin to match; a mouth with a smile she'd smother behind her hand when someone was being pompous or ridiculous, hiding her dimples; her flowing dark hair, and her walk, like a hidden dance.

Every time he pushed it—her—away. He had to be in command.

As darkness fell over the city he sat at his desk, eating a sandwich. He'd left the state dinner within minutes of the announcement of the royal engagement, pleading necessary business as a reason not to endure Amber's company. Or, more accurately, for her not to endure his company a moment longer than she needed to. He'd seen the look of surprise and slight confusion on her face, but again, he pushed it away.

His food slowly went stale as the mountain of papers slowly dwindled. He read each one carefully before signing, while dealing with necessary interruptions, the phone calls from various heads of state and security personnel.

In quiet moments, her face returned to his vision, but he always forced it out again.

Okay, so Amber was right; he hadn't looked at her much. What she didn't know was that he hadn't *dared* look at her. For weeks, months, he'd barely looked at her, never spoken beyond politeness, because he'd been too lost in shame that he hungered night and day for his brother's intended wife. Even her name had filled him with yearning: a precious jewel.

But never until yesterday had he dared think that she could ever become *his* jewel.

Lost and alone with his grief, unable to feel anything but pain, he'd been dazed when, out of nowhere, Sheikh Aziz wished him to become Amber's husband. He hadn't been able to say no. So close to breaking, he'd come to her today, touched by something he hadn't known in months, years...*hope.* Hope that even if she didn't feel the same, he wouldn't have to face this nightmare alone. Could it be possible that they might find comfort in one another, to stand together in this living death...?

And the overheard conversation was his reward for being so stupid. Of course Amber wanted Alim, his dashing brother, the nation's hero. As her father had said, what woman wouldn't want Alim?

A dream of twelve hours had now become his nightmare. There was no way out. She was stuck with him, the last option, the sheikh by default who didn't even want to be here.

What a fool. Hadn't he learned long ago that dreams were for other people? For Fadi, there had been his destiny as the next sheikh; for Alim, there was the next racing car, the next glamorous destination, the jets and the women and the adoration of his family and his nation. *Habib Abbas:* Alim was the country's beloved lion, their financial saviour since he'd found oil deep beneath the water of their part of the Gulf, and natural gas in the desert.

His parents would have been so proud of him. They'd always known Alim was destined for greatness, as Fadi had said so many times. *We're all so proud of you, Alim.*

Alim, the golden child. Of course he had Amber's heart—and of course he didn't want it. He'd thrown her away without a thought, just as he'd thrown his brother into his role of sheikh. He'd left them both to their fate without even a farewell or reason.

And yet, he still loved Alim; like everyone else in the country, he'd do anything for his brother. Alim knew that well, which was why he'd just disappeared without a word. 'Harun will do it better than I could, anyway,' had always been his casually tossed words when Fadi had needed him for one duty or another. 'He's good at the duty thing.'

Harun supposed he was good at it—he'd been raised to think his duty was sacred.

I never know what he's thinking or feeling. To her, he was Brother Number Three, nothing but an obligation, a means to enrich her country. She was only willing to marry him after being bullied and brought to a sense of pity for his grief by her father.

No, he had no choice but to marry her now—but he had no taste for his brother's unwanted leftovers. He'd dealt with enough broken hearts of the women who'd been rejected by Alim over the years, calling the palace, even offering themselves to him in the faint hope that he had the power to change Alim's mind.

Not this time. Never again. I might have to marry her, but I'll be damned if I touch her.

'It's lust, just lust,' he muttered, hard. Lust he could both deal with, and live without. Anything but the thought of taking her while she stared at the ceiling, wishing he were Alim—

His stomach burning, he found he was no longer hungry, and threw the rest of the sandwich into the garbage.

It was long past midnight before Harun at last

reached his rooms. He sent his hovering servants away and sat on his richly canopied bed, ripping the thin mosquito curtain. With an impatient gesture he flung it away; but if he made a noise, the bodyguards watching him from one of the five vantage points designed to protect the sheikh would come running in. So he sat looking out into the night as if nothing were wrong, and grieved in dry-eyed silence.

Fadi, my brother, my father! Allah, I beg you to let Alim live and return to me.

Three days later, the armed rebel forces of the el-Shabbat family invaded Sar Abbas.

CHAPTER TWO

Eight weeks later

'Habib Numara! Harun, our beloved tiger, our Habib Numara!'

Riding at the head of a makeshift float—two tanks joined by tent material and filled with flowers—Harun smiled and waved to the people lining the streets of Sar Abbas. Each cheering girl or woman in the front three rows of people threw another flower at him as he passed. The flowers landed on the float filling his nostrils until the sweet scent turned his stomach and the noise of the people's shouting left him deafened.

Still he smiled and waved; but what he wouldn't give to be in the quiet of his room reading a book. How had Alim ever endured this adulation, this attention for so many years? Fighting for his country, his men and repelling the el-Shabbat invasion—being wounded twice during battle, and having his shoulder put back in place after the dislocation—had been a positive relief in comparison to this.

You'll never be your brother.

Yet again his parents had been proven right. No, he'd never be like Alim.

As the float and the soldiers and the cheering throng

reached the palace he looked up. His future father-in-law stood beside his bride on the upper balcony, waving to him, looking proud and somehow smug. He supposed he'd find out why when he got some time.

Amber stood like a reed moving in the wind as she watched his triumphal entry. She had a small frown between her brows, a slight tilt to her head, as if trying to puzzle out something. As if she saw his discomfort and sympathised with him.

He almost laughed at the absurdity of the thought. She who loved Alim of racing fame and fortune, the real sheikh? *Right, Harun. She sees nothing in you but the replacement in her life and bed she'd do anything to avoid.*

She half lifted a hand. A smile trembled on her lips. Mindful of the people, he smiled and waved to his bride, giving her the public recognition and honour they expected.

It was all she wanted from him.

At last the wedding night she'd dreaded was upon her.

With a fast-beating heart, Amber stood in the middle of her bridal suite, with unbound hair, perfumed skin and a thin, creamy negligee over her nude body. So scared she could barely breathe, she awaited the arrival of her new husband.

The last of the fussing maids checked her hands and feet to be sure they were soft enough, perfumed to the right scent. Amber forced herself to stand still and not wave them off in irritation—or, worse, give in to her fears and ask someone, anyone what she must do to please a man she'd still barely spoken to. The way she felt right now, even the maid would do—for her mother had told her nothing. As she'd dressed her daughter for the marriage bed, the only words of advice to Amber had been, *Let your husband show you the way, and though it will hurt at first and you will bleed in proof of your virginity, smile and take joy in your woman's duty. For today, you become a woman.* And with a smile Amber didn't understand, she'd left the room.

In the Western world, girls apparently grew up knowing how to please a man, and themselves; but she'd been kept in almost total ignorance. In her world, it was a matter of pride for the husband to teach his wife what took place in the bed. No books were allowed on the subject, no conversation by the servants on the threat of expulsion, and the Internet was strictly patrolled.

She only wished she knew what to do…

More than that, she wished she knew him at all—that he could have taken an hour out of his busy schedule to get to know her.

In the end, she'd had the few months' wait she'd asked for, but it hadn't been for her sake, nor had they had any time to know each other better. The el-Shabbat family hadn't reckoned with Harun's swift action when they'd invaded the city. Handing the day-to-day work to his intended father-in-law, Harun had taken control of the army personally. Leading his men into battle using both the ancient and modern rules of warfare he'd learned since boyhood, Harun had gained the adoration of his people by being constantly in the thick of the fierce fighting, expecting and giving no quarter. The whispers in women's rooms were that he bore new scars on his body: badges of the highest honour. He'd spent no more than a night in the hastily erected Army hospital. Every time he'd been injured, come morning he'd returned to the battle without a word.

Within eight weeks he'd completely quelled the rebellion. By forgiving the followers of the el-Shabbat family and letting them return to their homes with little if any punishment and no public embarrassment, he'd earned their loyalty, his new title—and Amber's deep respect. By assuming control of the el-Shabbat fortune and yet caring for the women and children the dead enemy had left behind, he'd earned the love as well as the respect of his people.

If Alim was their beloved lion, Harun had become *Habib Numara,* their beloved tiger. 'It's a good omen for his marriage, with his bride coming from Araba Numara,' the servants said, smiling at her. 'It will be a fruitful union blessed by God.'

And in the weeks since then, as he'd put down the final shadows of the rebellion and with rare political skill brought together nation and people once more, Harun had had less time for her than Fadi had done. In fact he still barely spoke to her at all; but though he'd never said a word about his heroism on the field, he'd earned Amber's deep, reluctant admiration. If she still harboured regrets over Alim's disappearance, Harun's name now had the power to make her heart beat faster. He'd proved his worthiness without a word of bragging. She was ready to endure what she must tonight, and become the mother of his children.

As the main door opened the maid rushed to leave the room.

Sick to her stomach with nerves, she turned to where he stood—and her breath caught. It was strange, but it was only on the day she'd seen him returning to Sar Abbas as a national hero that she'd truly taken in his deep resemblance to Alim. A quiet, serious version, perhaps, but as, in his army uniform, he smiled and waved to the people cheering him in the streets, she'd seen his face as if for the first time.

Now, she struggled not to stare at him. So handsome and strong in his groom's finery, yet so dark and mysterious with those glittering forest-green eyes. She groped with one hand to the bedpost to gain balance suddenly lacking in her knees. He was the man who'd come home a hero. He was—magnificent. He was hers.

'None of you will listen or stand nearby,' he snapped at the walls, and she was filled with gratitude when she heard the shuffle of many feet moving away.

Lost in awe, she faltered in her traditional greeting, but bowed in the traditional show of deep respect. 'M-my husband, I…' She didn't know how to go on, but surely he'd understand how she felt?

Without a change of expression from the serious, cool appraisal, he closed the door behind him, and offered her a brief smile. 'Sit down, please, Amber.'

Grateful for his understanding, she dropped to the bed, wondering if he'd take it as a sign, or was she being too brazen? She only wished she knew how to go on.

He gave her a slow, thoughtful glance, taking in every inch of her, and she squirmed in embarrassment. Her heart beat like a bird trying to escape its cage as she waited for Harun to come to her, to kiss her or however it was this thing began. 'Well?' she demanded in a haughty tone, covering her rush of nerves with a show of pride, showing him she was worthy of him: a princess to the core. 'Do I pass your inspection, *Habib Numara?*'

For a moment, she thought Harun might actually smile as he hadn't done since the hero's return. There was a telltale glimmer in his eyes she'd noticed when he was in a rare, relaxed moment. Then, just as she was about to smile back, it vanished. 'You have to know you're a beautiful woman, Amber. Exquisite, in fact.'

'Thank you,' she whispered, her voice losing its power. He thought her exquisite? Something inside her melted—

He turned from her, and, drawing out a thin wreath of papers from a fold of his robe, sat at her desk. 'This should cover the necessary time. I forgot my pen, though. Do you happen to have one handy, my dear?'

Her mouth fell open as he began perusing whatever work he'd brought with him. He'd brought work to their wedding night? 'In the second drawer,' she responded, feeling incredibly stupid, but what else could she say?

'Thank you,' he replied, his tone absent. He pulled out one of her collection of pens and began reading, scrolling up and down the pages with his finger, and making notes in the margins.

She blinked, blinked again, unable to believe what she was seeing. 'Harun…' Then she faltered to a stop.

After at least ten seconds, he stopped writing. 'Hmm…? Did you say something, Amber?' His tone was the cold politeness of a man who didn't want to be disturbed.

'Yes, I did,' she retorted, furious. At least five different things leaped to her mouth. *What do you mean by covering the necessary time? What is it with the el-Kanar men? This is our wedding night!*

Don't you want me?

But at the thought of asking it, her confused outrage turned cold inside her, making her ache. *Why should this brother want me when the other two didn't?*

What's wrong with me?

But what came from her mouth, born of the stubborn pride that was her backbone in a world where she'd had beautiful clothes and surroundings but as much control over her destiny as a piece of furniture or a child's doll, she stated coldly, 'If there's no blood on the sheet tomorrow, the servants will talk. It will be around both our countries in hours. People will blame me, or worse, assume I wasn't a virgin. Will you shame me that way, when I've done nothing wrong?'

His back stiffened for a moment.

Amber felt the change in the air, words hovering on his lips. How she knew that about him, when they'd still barely spoken, she had no idea, but whatever he'd been about to say vanished in an instant.

'I see,' he said slowly, with only a very slight weariness in the inflection. 'Of course they will.'

He stood and stripped off his *kafta,* revealing his nakedness, and Amber's heart took wings again. Magnificent? Even with the scars across his back and stomach he was breathtaking, a battle-hardened warrior sheathed in darkest gold, masculinely beautiful and somehow terrifying. Involuntarily she shrank back on the bed, wishing she'd found another place to sit. *I'm not ready for this…please, Harun, be gentle with me…*

She couldn't breathe, watching him come to her.

But he walked around the bed as if she weren't there. He didn't touch her, didn't even *look* at her. At the other side of the bed, he put something down, and used both his hands to sweep all the rose petals from the coverlet. 'I don't like the smell. Cloying.'

'I like it,' she said, halfway between defiance and stupidity.

He shrugged and stopped brushing them away. 'It's your bed.' Then he lifted the thing he'd put on the bed: a ceremonial knife, beautifully scrolled in gold and silver.

'What's that…Harun…?' Her jaw dropped; she

watched in utter disbelief as he made a small cut deep in his armpit, and allowed a few drops of blood to fall into his cupped palm.

'What—what are you...?' Realising she was gaping, she slammed her mouth shut.

'Making a cut where it won't be seen and commented on,' he said in a voice filled with quiet irony. 'Thus I'm salvaging your pride in the eyes of others, my dear wife.'

'I don't understand.' Beyond pride now or remembering any of her instructions for tonight, she gazed at him in open pleading. 'What are you doing?'

He sighed. 'As you said, virgins bleed, Amber. It's my duty to ensure that your reputation isn't ruined. Pull the coverings down, please, and quickly, before the blood drops on the rug. Imagine what the servants would make of that.' His tone was filled with understated irony.

She closed her mouth and swallowed, and then swivelled around in the bed to pull the covers down.

She watched as he dripped blood into his other hand. 'It seems enough, I think,' he said after thirty seconds. Her husband of six hours looked at her. 'Which side of the bed do the servants know you prefer?'

Torn between shock and fury born of humiliation, she pointed.

'Thank you.' As casually as if he'd spilled water, he smeared his blood on the bed. Then he walked into the bathroom; she heard the sound of running water.

When he came out he returned to the desk, picked up his bridegroom's clothing, pulled it back over his head and let it fall to his feet. He sat down again, reading, scrolling and making notes.

Not knowing what else to do, she sat on the bed,

drawing her knees under her chin, her arms wrapped tight around them. And for the next hour, she watched him work in growing but helpless fury.

Why won't you touch me? she wanted to scream. *Why don't you want to touch me? What did I do wrong?*

But she'd made an innocent scene with Fadi when it was obvious he was running from her, and he'd told her about Rafa. *I can't marry her, but I love her, Amber.*

She'd made another scene before her father when Alim fled the country rather than marry her. *He has rejected both Fadi's position, and Fadi's bride.*

She was already the bad-luck bride in the eyes of the servants and the people—but if they found out about this, she'd never recover. Fadi had loved another; Alim fled the country—but neither of them had made the rejection this obvious.

Asking him why would only humiliate her further.

After a while, her husband said without looking at her, 'It would be best if you went to sleep, Amber. It's been a very long day for you.'

She lay back on the sheets, avoiding the smeared blood—but she kept watching him work out of a stubborn refusal to obey anything he asked of her. If he wasn't going to be a real husband, it relieved her of the necessity to be any kind of wife.

Suddenly she wondered how long a day it had been for him. How long had he been working—right up until he'd dressed for the wedding? During the ceremony and after he'd kissed her hand, touched her face with a smile, played the loving bridegroom—for the cameras and the people, no doubt. Now he was working again. Barely two months ago, Harun fought for his life, for the sake of a nation that didn't belong to him.

Did he ever stop, and just be a normal man?

Harun, just look at me, be kind to me for a minute.
I'm your bride, she wanted to say, but nothing emerged
from her mouth. She was lying on their marriage bed,
his for the taking in this shimmering piece of nothing,
and he was doing stupid paperwork.

He didn't even look at her, just as he never had before.

As a soldier, they said, he'd fought with a savagery
beyond anything they'd seen before. Like Fadi, had he
done it to escape her? What a shame for him that he'd
lived, forced into taking a wife he clearly didn't want
in the least.

She hated him. She hated this bed…and she couldn't
stand this ridiculous situation any more.

Pulling her hair into a messy knot, she got to her
feet, stalked into the bathroom, shredded the stupid
negligee in her haste to take it off, and scrubbed away
all traces of perfume and make-up under the stinging
heat of the shower.

Using the pumice stone she scrubbed at her skin
until it was raw, and took minimal comfort in the fact
that Harun would never know how he'd made her cry.

But as she scrubbed herself to bleeding point she
vowed she'd *never* make a fool of herself for an el-
Kanar man again. No, she'd show Harun nothing, no
emotion at all. She'd be a queen before him at all times,
damn it! And one day he'd come to her, on his knees,
begging for her…

If only she could make herself believe it.

CHAPTER THREE

Three Years Later

'My LADY, the Lord Harun has requested entrance!'

Startled, Amber dropped the papers she was reading and stared at her personal maid, Halala. Barely able to believe the words she'd heard, she couldn't catch her breath. All the ladies were in a flutter of excitement... and hope, no doubt.

She could almost hear the whispers from mouth to ear, flying around the palace. *Will he come to her bed at last?*

Her cheeks burned with embarrassment at the common knowledge within the palace of the state of her marriage, the tag of bad-luck bride she couldn't overcome, but she answered calmly enough. 'Please show my husband in, and leave us. I need not remind you of what will happen if you listen in,' she added sternly, holding each of her ladies-in-waiting with her gaze until they nodded.

As the room emptied she smoothed down her dress, her hair, while her pulse beat hard in her throat. What could he want? And she had no time to change out of one of her oldest, most comfortable dresses—

Then Harun entered her rooms, tall and broad-

shouldered, with skin like dark honey and a tiny cleft
in his chin; she'd long ago become accustomed to the
fact that her husband was a quiet, serious version of her
dashing first crush. But today his normally withdrawn
if handsome face was lit from within; his forest-at-dusk
eyes were alive with shimmering emotion, highlighting
his resemblance to Alim more than ever. 'Good morning, Amber,' he greeted her not quite formally, his intense eyes not quite looking at her.

He doesn't care what I'm wearing, Amber thought
in sullen resentment. How foolish she'd been for wishing to look pretty for him, even for a minute. *I don't
even know why I'm surprised. Or why it still hurts after
all this time.*

Why had her father wanted her to wed this—this
robot? He wasn't a man. He was barely human…at least
not where she was concerned. But, oh, she'd heard the
rumours that he was man enough for another.

She tamped down the weakness of anger, finding
strength in her pride. 'You need something, My Lord?'
she asked, keeping her tone meek, submissive, but just
as formal and distant as his. 'It must be important for
you to actually come inside my rooms. I believe this is
the first time you've come here willingly in three years.'

He looked at her then—with a cold flash in his eyes
that made her feel like a worm in dirt. 'Since you're
taking the gloves off, my wife, we both know it's the
first time I've been in here willingly at all, not merely
since our wedding night.'

The burning returned in full measure to her cheeks,
a stinging wave of embarrassment that came every time
she thought of that awful night. Turning from him with
insulting slowness, as if she didn't care, she drawled,
'You never did explain yourself.'

Yes, she'd said it well. As if it were a mere matter of curiosity for her, and not the obsession it had been for so long.

She marvelled that, in so long, there'd never been an opportunity to ask before—but Harun was a master at making certain they were never alone. His favourite place in the palace seemed to be his office, or the secret passageway between their bedrooms—going the other way, towards his room. Only once had she swallowed her pride, followed him out and asked him to come to her—

'I'm sure you've noticed that my life is rather busy, my wife. And really, there's no point in coming where you aren't welcome.'

The heat in her cheeks turned painful. 'Of—of course you're welcome,' she stammered. 'You're my husband.'

He shrugged. 'So says the imam who performed the service.'

Knowing what he'd left unsaid, Amber opened her mouth, and closed it. No, they weren't husband and wife, never had been. They hadn't even had one normal conversation, only cold accusation on her part, and stubborn silence on his.

Didn't he know how much it hurt that he only came to her rooms at night when the gossip became unbearable, and that he timed the hour and left, just as he had on their wedding night? Oh, she'd been cold and unwelcoming to him, mocking him with words and formal curtsies, but couldn't he see that it was only because she was unable to stand the constant and very public humiliation of her life? Every time he was forced to be near her she knew that soon, he'd leave without a word, giving her nothing but that cold, distant bow. And everyone in her world knew it, too.

'I didn't come here to start an argument.' He kept his gaze on her, and a faint thrill ran through her body, as delicious as it was unwelcome—yet Harun was finally looking at her, his eyes ablaze with life. 'Alim's shown up at last,' he said abruptly.

Amber gasped. Alim's disappearance from the clinic in Bern three years ago had been so complete that all Harun's efforts to find him had proven useless. 'He's alive?'

Harun nodded. 'He's in Africa, taken by a Sudanese warlord. He's being held hostage for a hundred million US dollars.'

Her hand fluttered to her cheek. 'Oh, no! Is he well? Have they hurt him?'

The silence went on too long, and, seeing the ice chips in his eyes, she realised that, without meaning to, she'd said something terribly wrong—but what?

Floundering for words when she couldn't know which ones were right or wrong, she tried again, wishing she knew something, anything about the man she'd married. 'Harun, what are you going to do about it?'

'Pay the ransom in full, of course. He's the true Sheikh of Abbas al-Din, and without the contracts from the oil he found we'd have very little of our current wealth.' He hesitated for a moment. 'I'm going to Africa. I have to be there when he's released, to find out if he's coming home. And—he's my brother.'

She'd expected him to say that, of course. From doing twelve hours of mind-numbing paperwork to meeting dignitaries and businessmen to taking up sword and gun, Harun always did what was right for the country, for his people, even for her, at least in public—but she hadn't expected the catch in his voice, or the shimmer of tears in those normally emotionless eyes. 'You love him,' she muttered, almost in wonder.

He frowned at her. 'Of course I do. He's my brother, the only family I have left, and he—might come home at last.'

The second catch in her stranger husband's voice made her search his face. She'd never seen him cry once since Fadi's death. He'd never seemed lonely or needy during the years of Alim's disappearance, at least not in her presence. But now his eyes were misty, his jaw working with emotion.

Amber felt a wave of shame. Harun had been missing his brother all this time, and she'd never suspected it. She'd even accused him once of enjoying his role too much as the replacement sheikh to care where Alim was, or if he was alive or dead. He'd bowed and left her without a word, seconds before she could regret her stupid words. She'd wanted to hurt him for always being so cold, so unfeeling with her—but during the past three years she'd been able to call or Skype with her family daily, or ask one sister or another to visit. She'd left him all alone, missing his brother, and she'd never even noticed until now.

The sudden longing to give him comfort when she knew he'd only push her away left her confused, even frightened. 'I'm sorry,' she said in the end—a compromise that was so weak, so wishy-washy she felt like an idiot. 'I hope he does come home, for your sake.'

'Thank you.' But it seemed she'd said the wrong thing again; the smile he gave her held the same shard of ice as his eyes. 'Will it make a difference to you?'

Taken aback, she stammered, 'W-what? How could Alim's return possibly make any difference to me?'

Harun shrugged, but there was something—a hint of fire beneath his customary ice with her. She didn't know why, but it fascinated her, held her gaze as if riveted to his face. 'He surrendered himself to the warlord in order to protect the woman who saved his life, a nurse working with Doctors for Africa. Very courageous of him, but of course one expects no less from the Racing Sheikh. Soon Alim will become the true, hereditary sheikh he should have been these three years, and I'll be back to being—Brother Number Three.'

By this point she wondered if any more blood could possibly pool in her face. Ridiculous that she could feel such envy for a woman she'd never met, but she'd always yearned to have a man care enough about her to make such a sacrifice. To know Alim, the man who'd run from *her,* could risk his life for another woman—

Then, without warning, Harun's deliberate wording slithered back into her mind like a silent snake, striking without warning. Frowning, she tilted her head, mystified. 'What did you mean by that—Brother Number Three?'

'It took you long enough to remember. Thinking of Alim, were you?' He lifted a brow, just a touch, in true understated irony, and, feeling somehow as if he'd caught her out in wrong behaviour, she blushed. Slowly, he nodded. 'I thought you might be.'

Her head was spinning now. 'You just told me he's alive and has been taken by a warlord. Who else should I be thinking about?' He merely shrugged again, and she wanted to hit him. 'So are you going to explain your cryptic comment?'

It took him a few moments to reply, but it wasn't truly an answer. 'You figure it out, Amber. If you think hard, you might remember…or maybe you won't. It probably was never very important to you.'

'I don't understand,' she said before she could stop herself.

His gaze searched hers for a few moments, but whatever he was looking for he obviously didn't find. For some reason she felt a sense of something lost she didn't know she'd had, the bittersweet wishing for what she never realised she could have had.

Before she could ask he shrugged and went on, 'By the way, you'll be needed for a telecast later today, of course, my dear. We're so glad Alim's alive, of course we're paying the ransom, et cetera.'

The momentary wistfulness vanished like a stone in a pond, only its ripples left behind in tiny circles of hurt. 'Of course,' she said mockingly, with a deep curtsy. 'Aren't I always the perfect wife for the cameras? I must be good for something, since you endure my continued barrenness.'

His mouth hardened, but he replied mildly enough, 'Yes, my dear, you're perfect—for the cameras.'

He'd left the room before the poison hidden deep inside the gently-spoken cryptic words hit her.

Brother Number Three.

Oh, no—had it been Harun standing behind the door when she'd discussed her unwanted marriage—no, her unwanted groom—with her father?

She struggled to remember what she'd said. The trouble was, she'd tried to bury it beneath a blanket of forgetfulness ever since she'd accepted her fate.

Brother Number Three…how am I to face this total stranger in the marriage bed?

Her father's words came back to haunt her. *He's been left completely alone…in deepest mourning…*

He'd heard everything, heard her fight with all her might against marrying him—

And he'd heard her father discuss her feelings for Alim.

She closed her eyes. Now, when it was far too late, she understood why her husband had barely spoken to her in all this time, had never tried to find friendship or comfort with her, had rarely if ever shown any emotion in front of her—and remembering how she'd reacted, then and just now…

For three years she'd constantly punished him for his reaction—one born of intense grief and suffering, a reaction she could readily understand…at least she could understand it now. During the most painful time of his life, he'd needed one person to be there for him. He'd needed someone not to abandon or betray him, and that was exactly what she'd done. He'd come to her that day, and she'd treated him with utter contempt, a most unwanted husband, when he'd been the one to salvage her pride and give her the honour she deserved.

No wonder he'd never tried to touch her, had never attempted to make love to her, even on the one occasion she'd gone to his room to ask him to come to her bed!

But had she asked? Even then she'd been so cold, so proud, not hesitating to let him know how he'd failed her over and over. *Give me a child and remove this shame you've forced on me all this time,* she'd said.

With a silent groan, she buried her face in her hands.

The question now was, what could she do to make him forgive her, when it was years too late to undo the damage?

* * *

Harun was climbing into the jet the next day when he heard his name being called in the soft, breathless feminine voice that still turned his guts inside-out.

She might be your wife, but she can't stand you. She wants Alim—even more, now she knows he's alive, and as heroic as ever.

The same old fight, the same stupid need. Nothing ever changed, including his hatred for his everlasting weakness in wanting her.

Lust, it's nothing more than lust. You can ignore that. You've done it for three years. After a few moments, struggling to wipe the hunger from his face, he turned to her. Afraid he'd give himself away somehow, he didn't speak, just lifted a brow.

With that limber, swaying walk, she moved along the carpet laid down for him to reach the jet from the limo, and climbed the stairs to him. Her eyes were enormous, filled with something he'd never seen from her since that wretched night a year ago when he could have had her, and he'd walked away. 'Harun, I want to come with you.'

A shard of ice pierced his heart. Amber hated to fly, yet here she was, ready to do what she hated most. For the sake of seeing Alim? 'No.'

She blinked and took an involuntary step back at his forceful tone. 'But I want to—'

He couldn't stand to hear her reasons. 'I said no.'

Her chin shot up then, and her eyes flashed. Ah, there was the same defiant wife he'd known and ached to have from three feet or three thousand miles of distance for so long. 'Damn you, Harun, it's all I'm asking of you.'

Harun turned his face away. Just looking at her right now hurt. For the first time she was showing him the impulsive, passionate side he'd believed slumbered deep inside her, and it was for Alim.

Of course it was for Alim; why should he expect anything else? In all these years, she'd only shown emotion once: when she'd asked—no, demanded—that he end her public shame, and give her a child. When he'd said no, she'd sworn at him for the first time.

But she'd just sworn at him again.

'You still care for him so much?' he asked, his voice low and throbbing with the white-hot betrayal he barely managed to hide.

She sighed. 'I'm not nineteen any more. I'm your wife. Please, just give me a chance. It's all I'm asking.'

A chance for what? he wanted to ask, but remained silent.

Something to the left of him caught his attention. Her bags were being stowed in the hold. With a sense of fatalism, he swept a hand before him. 'By all means, come and see him. I'm sure he'll appreciate your care.'

No part of her touched him as she pushed past him and into the jet. Her chin was high, her eyes as cold as they'd always been for him...except on that fateful night last year—and a moment ago, because she wanted to see Alim.

Damn her. Damn them both.

Yet something like regret trailed in the wake of the warm Gulf wind behind her. Harun breathed it in, refusing to yet again indulge in the wish that things could be different for them. It was far too late.

She was sitting upright and straight in the plush, wide seat, her belt already buckled. He sat beside her, and saw her hands gripping the armrests. He'd seen this on the times they'd had to go to another country for a state visit. She really hated flying.

His hand moved to hers, then stopped. It wasn't his comfort she wanted.

During the final safety check of the jet the silence stretched out. The awkwardness between them was never more evident than when they sat side by side and could find nothing to talk about: he because all he could think of was touching her and hating himself for it, and she presumably because all she wanted was to get away from him, as fast and as far as possible.

How she must hate this life, trapped in this submissive woman's role, tied to a man she despised.

'You are *not* Brother Number Three.'

Startled, he turned to face her, prompted by a tone of voice he'd never known from his cold, proud wife. The fierce words seemed to burst from her; the passion he'd always felt slumbering in her came to blazing life in a few restrained words. 'I'm sorry I ever said it, and sorrier still that you heard stupid words said in my own shock and grief, and took them so literally. I humiliated you before my father, and I'm sorry, Harun.'

Surprise and regret, remembered humiliation, yearning and a dozen other emotions flew around in him, their edges hitting him like the wings of a wild bird caged. He could only think of one thing to say, and he couldn't possibly say it to his stranger wife. *What am I to you now?* As ever, he resorted to his fall-back, the cool diplomacy that told her nothing about what he was thinking or feeling. 'It's all right.'

'No, it isn't. It's not all right between us. It never has been, and I never knew why. But we've been married for three years. In all this time, why didn't you try, even once, to talk to me?' Touching his cheek, she turned him to face her before he could school his stunned surprise that her hands were on his skin. 'I always wanted to know why you hated me. You were outside the door that day.'

Taken aback, he could only answer with truth. 'I don't hate you.'

An encyclopaedia could be written on the doubt in her eyes. 'Really? You don't?'

Reluctant understanding touched a heart shrouded in ice too long. 'No,' was all he said.

She sighed. 'But you don't trust me. You won't treat me even as a friend, let alone your wife.' She shook her head. 'I thought you were a servant when I heard your footsteps behind the door. I would never have done that to you—don't you know that?'

Her face was vivid with the force of her anger and her regret. She thought she wanted to know about his emotions—but she didn't have a clue. If he let out one iota of his feelings, it might break a dam of everything he'd repressed since he was eight years old.

I need you to be strong for me again, little akh, Fadi had said at his mother's funeral, only three months after their father died, and Alim had stormed off within minutes of the service beginning. *We have to stand together, and show the world what we're made of.*

I need you to stay home and help me, little akh, he'd said when Alim was seventeen, and his first race on the circuit gave him the nickname the Racing Sheikh. *What Alim's doing could change the nation for us, economically and socially. You can study by correspondence, right? It won't make a difference to you.*

I need you to come home, little akh. I feel like I'm drowning under the weight of all this, Fadi had said when Harun was nineteen, and had to go on a dig to pass his archaeology course. *I'll fix it with the univer-*

sity, don't worry. You'll pass, which is all you want, right?

'I suppose I should have known,' he answered Amber now. From the vague memories he had of his mother, he knew that it was dangerous not to answer an angry woman, but it was worse to answer with a truth she didn't want to hear.

'And—and you heard what my father said about—' her cheeks blazed, but her chin lifted again, and she said it '—about the—the feelings I had for Alim back then.'

As a passion-killer, hearing his wife say she had *feelings* for the brother who'd abandoned him to this half-life had to rank up there as number one. 'Yes,' he said, quiet. Dead inside.

'Harun, don't.' She gripped his chin in her hand, her eyes fairly blazing with emotion. 'Do you hate me for it?'

He closed his eyes against the passion always beneath the surface with her, but never for him. 'No.' So many times, he'd wished he could hate her, or just take her for the higher duty of making an heir, but he could do neither. Yes, he still desired her; he could live with that. But he'd shut off his heart years ago. There was no way he'd open it up, only to have her walk all over it again with her careless rejections and stinging rebukes.

'Stop it, Harun,' she burst out, startling him into opening his eyes again. 'Hate me if you want, but stop showing me this uncaring wall of ice! I don't know how to talk to you or what to do when you're so cold with me, always pushing me away!'

Cold? He felt as if he were bleeding agony whenever he looked at her, and she thought his feelings for her were cold? Harun stared at her, the wife he barely knew, and wondered if she was blind, or if it was because he really had covered his need too well. But wasn't that what he'd always done? How could he stop doing what had always been expected of him?

So he frowned again. 'I don't know what you want me to say.'

'Talk to me for once. Tell me how it hurt you.' Though she spoke softly, almost beneath her breath, it felt like a dam bursting, the release of a long-held pressure valve. 'I was *nineteen,* Harun, one of a legion of girls that dreamed of capturing the heart of the world-famous Racing Sheikh. I didn't know him any more than I could touch or talk to a literal star.'

She hadn't said so many words to him at one time since he'd rejected her one attempt at connection last year—and the bitter self-mockery in her voice and her eyes lashed even harder at him than herself.

So she thought of Alim as a star. Well, why not? Even now, years later, it was how the world saw him. The headlines were filled with adoring references to the missing sheikh, reinforcing his own aching emptiness. *He's my brother. Not one of you misses him like I do.*

When he didn't answer, she snapped, 'Do you feel nothing about it, Harun? Do you not care that I married you believing I was in love with your brother?'

The pain of it gripped him everywhere, like a vice inside him, squeezing the blood from his heart. Not care that she—

Believing she was in love with Alim? What did she mean?

Did he want to know? Could he stand to ask what she felt for his brother now?

This was too much. She'd changed so suddenly from the cold, imperious woman she'd always been with him; it left him wondering what the hell to say to her that wouldn't make her explode. After three years of icy disdain and silence, without warning she was demanding thoughts and feelings from him that threatened to take the only thing he had left; his pride.

'Of course I cared,' he said coolly. 'Quite humiliating, isn't it, to be the last brother in line in the eyes of your prospective bride—good old Brother Number Three. I didn't enjoy knowing that my wedding only took place because one brother died and the other brother ran away. Worse still to know she'd have done anything to have my runaway brother there instead of me.' He was quite proud of himself. Total truth in a few raw sentences, years of grief, loss and anguish— but told as if it were someone else's life, as if it didn't twist in his guts like a knife he couldn't pull out of him.

The fire in her eyes dimmed. 'I suppose it is,' she said dully. 'Thank you for your honesty, at least.'

And, too late, Harun knew he'd blown this last chance she'd given him to connect with her. She might have said and done it all wrong, but at least she was trying.

I never know what he's thinking or feeling.

For years the words had haunted him, leaving him locked deep inside what had always been his greatest strength—but with Amber, it felt like his deepest inadequacy. He'd grown up always aware that, hereditary sheikh though he was, he was the last in line, the spare tyre, the reliable son or brother. His parents had been busy running a nation, too busy to spend time with their children. The only memories he had of his mother was that she'd resented that the last child she could have wasn't the girl she'd longed for. His father, who wanted sons, contemptuously called him a sissy for his love of history and hiding in his room reading books instead of playing sports and inventing marvellous things as Alim could, or charming the people, as Fadi did. *He'll grow up to be a real man whether he likes it or not,* their father said with utter disdain when Harun was six. From that day, he'd been enrolled in all the action-man activities and ancient and modern knowledge of war-craft that made the family so popular with the people.

He'd learned to fight, all right…he'd had no choice, since his father had arranged constant martial-arts battles for him. But he'd also read books late at night, beneath the blanket with a tiny hand-torch, so the servants wouldn't see it and report to his father.

After their parents' deaths, Fadi had become the father he'd never known, raising both his brothers with greater love and acceptance than Harun had ever known from his parents, and yet he'd had to learn how to run the small, independent emirate. Harun adored Fadi, and Fadi had always loved him dearly, giving him the affection he'd craved for so long; but Fadi always comforted himself in the knowledge that, while Alim would travel the world, and put Abbas al-Din on the world and economic map, Harun would stay home and help.

Alim had always counted on it, too. *You've got Harun,* Alim would always say when Fadi asked him to come home for this duty or that. *He'll do it better than I can.*

So Harun supported Fadi's heavy load as Sheikh, kept learning war-craft and how to lead all the armed forces, continuing the studies that were his secret passion by reading books late at night. Since he'd been recalled home at nineteen from his one trip outside the palace, he'd never dreamed of asking to leave Sar Abbas, except on matters of military or state. His interests were unimportant beside the demands of nation, honour, family, and their people. Good old Harun, doing the right, the decent and honourable thing, always his brothers' support and mainstay.

The thing was, nobody ever asked him how he felt about it, or believed he had feelings at all. And so, as long as he could remember, he'd kept his thoughts to himself.

So how did he suddenly begin talking now, after all these years?

Amber sighed aloud, reiterating his failure with her. 'Say something, *anything,* Harun!'

What was he supposed to say? 'I'm sorry, Amber.' At this moment, he wished he'd realised how very young she'd been when they wed—as she'd said, only nineteen. He sat beside this wife who despised him, feeling the old chains of silence holding him in place, with a rusted padlock he could never seem to open.

'If it ruined everything we could have had, I wish I'd never thought of Alim,' she burst out, yet said it very quietly. She dropped his hand, and turned away. 'I never even knew him, but I was all alone here. Fadi loved Rafa, and you never looked at me or talked to me. And—and he smiled and was nice to me when he came. It was just a lonely girl's stupid crush on a superstar,' she mumbled, her cheeks aflame.

The finality in her words dropped him into a well of unexpected darkness. *Don't you understand, Amber? If he'd been anyone else, I could have ignored it.* 'What could we have had, Amber?' he asked, as quietly as she'd spoken.

Her left shoulder lifted in a delicate shrug. 'We married because you were a sheikh and I was a sheikh's daughter, for the sake of our nations. Harun, you've been so amazing the past three years. You've been a strong and loving leader for your people in their need, giving them everything they asked of you. But the only good part of our marriage was for the cameras and in front of the people. Now, if Alim comes back—well, what's left for us?'

Us. She'd said *us.* As if there were an *us*—or could have been. She'd admired him for the things he'd done? He couldn't get his head around it.

'I don't want a sham for the cameras any more. I don't want to live the rest of my life alone, tied to a man who never touches me, who doesn't want me.'

Harun had never cursed his habit of silence more than now. Strong, brave, lovely Amber had burst out with everything they'd kept locked in silence all these years, and his mind was totally blank. He'd been too busy keeping his nation intact and his heart from bearing any more scars to say a word to her about his wants and needs, and he'd presumed she didn't care what he wanted anyway, because she still loved Alim.

But if that wasn't the truth, why had she walled off from him so completely? He'd thought it was because she found him repulsive—but now?

But last year, she'd come to him. She'd asked him to make love to her…

'I never knew you wanted me to desire you,' he said, fighting the husky note of long-hated yearning with all he had. His pride had taken enough battering from this woman, and he'd been celibate far too long. *Say it, Amber, tell me if you want me—*

But with a jerky movement Amber unlocked her seat belt and got to her feet. Her eyes blazed down at him, thwarted passion burning bright. 'Can't you just talk to me like you're a normal man, and show me some human feeling? Can't you stop—stop fencing with words, asking questions instead of answering me honestly? Can't you stop being so cold all the time? I'm not your enemy, I'm your *wife!*'

Stop reading books, Harun! Stop saying yes and do it, be a real man like your brothers!

He rubbed at his forehead in frustration. 'Amber, stop talking in circles and tell me what you want,' he grated, knowing he sounded harsh but no longer caring. He felt as if he had enough to deal with right now without her baffling dramatics. Couldn't she see that she was expecting too much, too fast? 'Can we do this thing later? In a few hours I'll be facing my brother for the first time in years. Alim's my only family, all I have left.'

'It only needed that.' With a slow nod, those beautiful, liquid-honey eyes iced over, frozen in time like her namesake. 'We don't have to do this *thing* at all. Thank you, Harun. You've made my decision easy.' And she walked—that beautiful swaying dance she put into every effortless step—into the cockpit and asked in a voice as curt as her walk had been shimmering, 'I don't want to go now. Open the exit door, please.'

When it was open, she moved to the exit, her head high. At the opening, she turned—only her head—and glanced at him. She spoke with regal dignity, the deposed queen she was about to become. 'I hope your reunion with Alim is all you wish it to be. I hope he comes home to be your family.'

He opened his mouth, but she rushed on, as if unable to bear hearing his formal thank-you. 'When Alim becomes the sheikh again, I hope you find what you want out of your life. I hope you find a way to be happy,

Harun, because I'm going to find my own life from now on, without you or anyone else telling me what to do.'

Then, like a dream of beauty abruptly awakened, she was gone.

CHAPTER FOUR

Fifteen Days Later
The Sheikh's Palace, Sar Abbas

HARUN had asked Amber to be here at this private handover of the nation to the real Sheikh of Abbas al-Din, and so she'd come, from curiosity if nothing else—but it seemed as if nobody else would begin speaking, so she'd have to.

Maybe that was what Harun wanted from her, to break the ice?

Right now she felt as if she'd give anything to be able to do just that—to break the ice of Harun's withdrawn politeness. In the last fifteen days she'd come to regret her outburst. When would she learn to control her tongue and temper? Neither had got her anywhere with the el-Kanar brothers, least of all Harun.

'Welcome home, Alim,' she said, trying to smile, to repress the emotion boiling like a pot beneath the surface. 'It's good to have you back.'

Her long-lost brother-in-law looked older than the handsome, daring racing driver she remembered. The scars on his face and neck, the mementoes of the race that took Fadi's life, weren't as bad as she'd feared. He was still the kind of man who'd draw admiring looks from women wherever he went, though, from the wariness in his stance when any woman was nearby, she suspected he didn't know it.

Alim flicked a glance at Harun, but he stood impassive, neither moving nor speaking. After a few moments Alim bowed to her, a smile on his mouth as stressed as the look in his eyes. 'Thank you, Amber.'

It seemed the charming daredevil who'd grabbed her youthful fancy was gone—like her long-disappeared crush. But this man was her brother-in-law, a stranger to her—and this was not her reunion. So she waited, casting small glances about the room. The awkward tension between the brothers was too hard to keep watching.

This beautiful, airy but neutral room was almost as hard to look at. This had been Fadi's reception room to meet foreign dignitaries, and it was where she'd met all three el-Kanar brothers for the first time. The dear friend who'd loved another woman, the glamorous racing hero who'd disappeared rather than wed her, and the man of ice who'd done his duty by her in public, but would do anything rather than talk to her or touch her.

Harun must have noticed that she and Alim were both awaiting their cue from him. He spoke with an odd note in his voice. 'I've moved out of your room, Alim. It's ready for you, as is your office, as soon as you want to resume your duties.'

Alim took a step towards his brother. 'Let's not pretend. Don't talk as if I've been sick for a few weeks. I was gone for three years. I left all the grief and duty to you. Harun, I wanted to say that…'

Harun shrugged, with all his eloquent understatement, and she realised he did it with Alim, not just with her. It seemed he was skilled at cutting off more people than her alone. He shut off anyone's attempts at emotional connection, freezing them out with that hint of blue-blooded frost. *Come no further.* 'There's no need to say anything, Alim. It wasn't as if I had anywhere better to be at the time.'

But Alim wasn't having it. With a determined tone, he went on, 'I wanted to say, the choice is yours now. You've done a magnificent job of running the country, of picking up the pieces after Fadi's death and my disappearance. You're the nation's hero now, not me. If you want to remain the sheikh—'

'No.'

The snarl burst from her mouth, shaking her to the core, but it had a masculine note as well. Harun had echoed it even more forcefully than she had; he sounded almost savage.

Amber felt Alim staring at her, waiting. Maybe it was easier for him to hear her out first than to know what he'd done to Harun by his disappearance.

She flushed, and glanced at Harun—but as usual, he stood locked inside those walls of silence she couldn't knock down, even with catapults and cannons.

She fiddled with her hands, shuffled a foot. Did she want to hear Harun's reasons for wanting out before she'd spoken? Suddenly she couldn't bear to know, to hear all the reasons why she'd failed him, and heard words tumbling from her lips.

'I won't play sheikh's happy wife for anyone's sake any more. I'm tired of the pretence that everything's all right. I don't care what my father says. I want a divorce.'

She turned and walked out of the room, trying to contain the trembling in every part of her body. She reached her suite of rooms and closed the door behind her. It almost felt like a miracle to make it this far without being stopped, but she'd managed it by staring down anyone that approached her. She encountered more than twenty people, staffers or servants, all asking if they could serve her—all burning to know the answer to one question. Who was the sheikh now, Alim or Harun?

Sitting on the straight-backed chair at her desk, she counted in silence. If he didn't come this time—

In less than three minutes, the door swung wide open without announcement. 'Guard every possible listening place, but stay well away from it,' Harun snapped to someone outside, and several masculine voices lifted in assent. From behind the walls of her suite, she heard the soft shuffling of feminine feet moving away in haste, and smiled to herself.

'He comes to my rooms twice in a month of his own free will,' she murmured, as if to herself. 'Will the walls fall flat in shock?'

Harun's gaze narrowed. 'Is that really how you want to conduct this conversation, Amber, in sarcasm and anger?'

She lifted her chin. 'If it actually makes you feel something, I'll risk it.'

'You needn't worry about that,' he said grimly. 'I'm feeling quite a lot of things right about now.'

'Then I'm glad,' she said with sweet mockery. It seemed the only way to break through that invisible, impenetrable wall of concrete around him.

And it worked. With a few steps he was right in front of her, his chest rising and falling in abrupt motion, his normally forest-green eyes black with intensity. The emotion she'd hungered to see for so long had risen from his self-dug grave and the satisfaction hit her like a punch to the stomach. 'How dare you make an announcement like that with my brother there?'

'I had to,' she said with false calm, heart hammering.

'Without him there it would have done no good, because it seems to me that you don't care what I say or what I think. You've never once asked or cared what I want. What's right for Abbas al-Din is all that matters to you.'

Ah, why did there have to be that little catch in her voice, giving her away?

But it seemed he didn't even notice it. 'He wants to marry the nurse that rescued him. He loves her, just so you know,' he replied in a measured, even tone—but the fire in his eyes showed the struggle he was having in commanding his emotions.

Incensed, she jerked to her feet. 'Is that all you can say? I tell you I want a divorce, and you only want to remind me of a stupid crush I had when I was nineteen? How long will you keep punishing me for words I said and feelings I had when I was barely out of childhood? I was grieving too, you know. I cared for Fadi. He was like a big brother to me.' Afraid she'd burst into unseemly tears in front of him, she wheeled away, staring hard out of that beautifully carved window, blinking the stinging from her eyes. She'd rather *die* than cry in front of him. 'I've always known I meant nothing to you beyond the political gain to your country, but I hoped you respected me a little more than that.'

The silence stretched out so long, she wondered if he'd left. He had the knack of moving without sound. Then he spoke. 'You're right. I apologise, Amber.' As she whirled around he gave her a small smile. 'I had my own stupid crush at nineteen—but I didn't marry you while I was in love with your sister. Do you understand?'

They were the first words he'd ever spoken that felt real to her, and she put a hand on the chair to feel something solid; the truth had hit her that hard. She'd thought of it as a silly crush on a superstar all this time—but Alim was his brother. Though he'd said it simply, it sickened her. She'd married him with a crush on his *brother*—the brother that had publicly humiliated her. As far as deeply personal insults went, it probably couldn't get much worse.

'I understand,' she said, her voice croaky.

He nodded. 'We both know you can't divorce me, Amber. It would bring dishonour on the family and threaten the stability of the country, so I don't believe that was what you want most.'

Hating that he'd called her on her little power-game, she said wearily, 'I don't have to live here, Harun.' She rubbed her eyes, heedless of make-up. What did it matter what she looked like? He didn't want her, had never wanted her.

His jaw hardened. 'You'd make our problems public by leaving me?'

'I was never *with* you to leave you, My Lord. The little scar in your armpit is evidence enough of that.' But instead of feeling triumph at the taunt, she just wanted to cry. Why did she always have to attack? And why did it take attacking him to make him *talk?*

'So you're saying you'll drag us both through the mud by proving I didn't consummate the marriage?'

She lifted her face, staring at him in disbelief. 'Is that all you care about—if I embarrass you in public? When you've been humiliating me publicly for years!' she flung at him. 'Everyone in the palace knows you don't come to my bedroom! I'm known as the bad-luck bride, who's ruined the lives of all three el-Kanar brothers. Even my parents bemoan my inability to entice you—not to mention the lack of grandchildren— every time they visit or call me!' She was quite proud of herself, laying her deepest, bleeding wound before him with such flaming sarcasm instead of crying or wailing like a weak woman. 'And of course everyone's very well aware your lack of interest must be my fault, since our wedding night was apparently consummated, and you never came back.' She paused, and looked at him reproachfully, before delivering the final blow. 'Oh, and nobody in the palace has hesitated to tell me about your lover and daughter. Do you know how it feels to know that while you continue to leave me alone, you gave another woman the only thing I've ever asked of you—and even the servants know about it?'

Harun closed his eyes and rubbed his forehead, shoulders bent. He looked unutterably weary, and part of her ached to take the words back, to make this conversation any time but now. 'I would have thought you'd know by now that servants only ever get things half-right. The child's name is Naima. Her mother is Buhjah, and she's a good woman.' His words were tight, locking her out again.

Amber stared in disbelief. She'd just bared her greatest shame to him, the very public and family humiliation she had to endure daily, and he could only speak of his daughter and lover—the family he'd allowed her to learn about from the servants?

Did he love Buhjah? Was that why he'd never cared how she felt or what she needed? Just like Fadi, all over again. Oh, these el-Kanar brothers were so faithful to the women they loved. And so good at doing their public duty by her and then leaving her in no-man's-land, stuck in a life she could no longer bear.

'Get out,' she said, her voice wobbling. She wheeled away, her breast heaving with her choppy breathing. 'Just go. Oh, and you'd better lock me in, because it's the only way your precious name won't be dragged through the mud you're so afraid of.'

'No, I won't leave it like this,' he said, hard and unbending. Oh, no, he wouldn't plead, not with her. Probably the mother of his child roused his gentleness and touch and had the man on his knees for her. For Amber, there was only an unending wall of ice. But then, why should she expect more? She was only the wife.

She buried her face in her hands. 'Oh, by all means, master, stay, and force me to keep humiliating myself before you. You're in control by law and religion. I can't stop you.' The words scraped across a throat as raw as the desert, but she no longer cared. It wasn't as if he gave a fig if she did weep or how she felt about anything—but the embarrassment at her less than regal behaviour might just get rid of him for a little while.

'Amber, I don't want to keep going like this. I can see you're hurting, but I don't know how to help you.'

Seconds later she heard the door close softly behind him, and heaved a sigh—whether in relief or from the greatest misery she'd ever known, she wasn't sure. Had she got her point across to him at last, or had she driven him away?

There would be no divorce. Her father would see her dead before he'd allow it, and she couldn't just disappear. Even if she weren't hemmed in by servants, she'd put her family through public shame, the scandal would leave her younger sisters unmarriageable and, worst of all, she'd have to leave her family behind for ever.

Unthinkable. Impossible. They were all she had, and, despite her ongoing conflicts with her father, she loved them all dearly.

So she was stuck here, for ever bound to this man—

'So why do I keep driving him away?' she muttered through her fingers. If she wanted any kind of amity in her life—and, most importantly, a child to fill the hole in her heart and end her public shame—she had to let Harun know the truth. That, far from hating him, she punished him for his neglect of her because she admired and desired him, and had since before their wedding day. Even now she pushed him in some desperate attempt to get him to really speak to her, to feel something, anything—

No. She'd die before she told him. He had to give her some sign first! But how to—?

The rag crossed her mouth with shocking suddenness. Panic clawed at her and she struggled, but within moments it was tied at the back of her head. Another bound her hands together behind her. She kept fighting, but then a sickly sweet stench filled her nostrils, and made her head spin before everything turned black.

Three steps from her door, Harun stopped and wheeled around. What was he doing?

Amber was crying, and he'd left her. He'd never believed he'd ever have the power to make her cry, but he had…talking of Naima and Buhjah—

'Idiot!' he muttered when at last a light went on in his brain and his heart after years of darkness. Was it possible? Could Amber be jealous? He struggled to think. Did she yearn for the child she'd demanded of him last year, the child he'd never given her—his children that were her right as his wife…or—dear God in heaven…he'd let her keep thinking Buhjah was Rafa's real name—that she was his lover, not Fadi's—

Amber was his wife. He owed her his first loyalty, not Buhjah and Naima, much as he cared for both of them. He owed Amber a lot more than the public presence he gave her. And—what if all her roundabout talking, her probing and proud demands for more than the child she'd asked him for a year ago were supposed to help him to work out that she wanted more? That she wanted him?

He stalked back through the door before he could change his mind. 'Amber, I'm not going anywhere—'

Then he jerked to a standstill, staring at the sliding door of the secret passage that joined the back of their bedrooms—the one that was never watched, at his strict order. It led to freedom through a tunnel below the palace, created during the seventeenth century, when many brides were taken by abduction. Amber's feet were all he saw as the door began to slide closed again, but they were sliding backwards.

Someone had her! If it was the el-Shabbats…or worse, the more virulent of the el-Kanar supportive factions who'd kept sending him messages to rid himself of her, that she was bad luck—dear God, the return of Alim might have spurred them to action. The faction of reactionary, old-fashioned autocrats hated Alim for his western ways, and wanted to keep Harun as Sheikh. If they'd taken Amber, they'd use her as leverage to make Alim disappear for good—and then they'd kill her to leave Harun free to wed a more fertile bride.

No!

'Amber!' he yelled, bolting for the door. He reached it before it slid shut, yanked it open and shouldered his way through.

Turning left, he ran down the passage—then a cloying scent filled his senses and mind; the world spun too fast, and he knew no more.

CHAPTER FIVE

THE screaming headache and general feeling of grogginess were the first indications that life wasn't normal when Harun opened his eyes…because when he tried to open them they were filled with sticky sand, and he had to blink and push his lids wide before they opened.

The second indication was when he saw the room he was in. Lying on a bed that—well, it *sagged,* he could feel his hip aching from the divot his body had made— he knew this was a room he'd never been in before. It wasn't quite filthy, but for a man who'd spent every day of his life in apartments in flawless condition, he could smell the dust, breathe it in.

The furnishings were strange. After a few moments of blinking and staring hard, he thought he hadn't been in a room so sparse since his tent during the war. The one cupboard looked as though it had been sanded with steel wool, the gouges were so messy, and it was old. Not antique, but worn out, like something sold at a bazaar in the poor quarter of the city. The one carpet on the wide-boarded wooden floor looked like an original eighteenth-century weave, but with moth-holes and ragged ends. The dining table and chairs had been hand-carved in a beautiful dark wood, but looked as if they hadn't been polished in years. The chairs by the windows were covered in tapestry that had long lost its plushness.

Thin, almost transparent curtains hung over the wide, ornately carved windows and around the bed, giving an illusion of privacy; but in a life filled with servants and politicians, foreign dignitaries and visiting relatives, he barely understood what the word meant.

He moved to rub his eyes, but both hands came together. His hands were tied with a double-stranded silken string. Could he break it if he struggled hard enough—?

The silk was stronger than it appeared. The bonds didn't budge, no matter how he struggled, and he swore.

A little murmur of protest behind him made him freeze halfway through pulling his wrists apart. A soft sigh followed, and then the soft breathing of a woman in deep sleep.

He flipped his body around to the other direction, his head screaming in protest at the movement, and looked at his companion. Pale-faced, deeply asleep, Amber was in bed with him for the first time, wearing only a peignoir of almost the same shimmering honey-gold as her skin.

For that matter, he wore only a pair of boxers in silk as thin as Amber's peignoir.

A memory as blurry as a photo of his grandparents' youth came to him—a vision of Amber's feet being dragged backwards down the secret passage. But, try as he might, nothing more came to him.

They'd obviously been kidnapped, but why? For money, or political clout? Why would anyone want to take them now, when it was too late? It made no sense, with Alim back and able to take his rightful place as Sheikh—

Unless…could this be part of an elaborate el-Shabbat plot to reduce the el-Kanar power base in Abbas al-Din? He'd just paid one hundred million US dollars for Alim's safe release. If Alim paid the same for his and Amber's safe return, it wouldn't bankrupt the nation, but it would be enough to create a negative media backlash against the family. *Why do these people keep getting kidnapped?* Once was forgivable, but twice would be seen as a family weakness. If they'd taken Alim as well, it might destroy the—

An icy chill ran down his back. If it was the el-Shabbats, it would mean their deaths, all of them. Alim had just been taken hostage, beaten badly, and released only by ransom. How could he stand it again so soon? If Alim was taken or, God forbid, dead—his only brother, the only one he had left in the world—

He had to get out of here! When a guard came in, he'd be ready. He jerked to a sitting position, looking around the room for something, anything that could be used as a weapon.

Amber's tiny murmur of protest let him know he'd disturbed her. He dragged in a slow breath, taking a few moments to reorient himself. If anything had happened to Alim, right now he couldn't do a thing about it. Getting Amber out safely had to be his first priority—but even if they managed to escape, how could they reach home, almost completely undressed?

He'd wondered what kind of kidnapper would put him on a bed dressed in almost nothing, lying beside his scantily clad wife, but now he saw the point all too well. Without clothes, with no dignity, what could he do?

Find some clothes—and I will find a way out of here.

Slowly, gently, he got to his feet, making a face at the swishing slide of the shorts against his skin. He wore silk clothes only for ceremonial occasions, preferring cotton. Jeans and T-shirts had been his favoured fashion in his private time, until it had been made clear to him that, as replacement sheikh, he had to be seen to be the perfect Arabic man at all times.

With only two rooms, searching their cage didn't take long. Besides the bed, the dining set, the chairs by the windows, and the cupboard, there was only a prayer mat. He realised that was what had woken him, the call to prayer being made somewhere behind the building.

But even with his hands tied, he could look around.

The massive double door was locked. The only other doors, to the bathroom and the balcony, showed no chance of escape. The room they were in was five storeys up, without convenient roofs nearby to leap onto. Even if there were, he couldn't ask Amber to leap from one roof to another, and he couldn't leave her alone to face the consequences of his escape.

On the bedside tables were water glasses, and paper tissues. In the drawer on Amber's side there were about twenty hairpins.

They even knew how she preferred to do her hair, he thought grimly.

He crawled awkwardly under the bed, finding only dust. Using both hands together, he opened the cupboard—nothing at all but the hanging rail.

That had possibilities, if only he could get it out. But pulling and tugging at the rail made his head spin.

He checked through the bathroom, including the two small cupboards there. Even the most basic of bathroom goods could be used together to create something to help them escape.

'No floss, not even toilet paper in here,' he muttered moments later, resisting the urge to slam a cupboard, or throw one of the little bottles of oil at the wall. 'What kind of crazy kidnappers give their captives scented oils for their bath?'

Then his mind began racing. With the right oils, combined with the toothpaste and some water—he assumed they'd be fed and given water, at least—he might be able to make something…perhaps one of Alim's infamous stink-bombs from childhood, or some kind of fluid to throw in their kidnappers' eyes.

How he wished he'd paid more attention to Alim's scientific pranks when they were kids!

The bathroom held no more secrets. The bath was old and large, scrubbed clean. The toilet had a hose beside it. The towels were close to threadbare, useless for anything but basic drying. Their abductors weren't taking any chances.

He'd run out of options for now. With a clenched jaw, Harun let the pounding of his head and eyes dictate to him. He fell back on the bed, closed his eyes and breathed in the scent she wore. Intoxicating as an unfurled desert bud, soft and tender as a mid-spring night—was it perfume or the essence of Amber herself? He wished he knew. Drinking it in with each breath, savouring an intimacy so new and yet somehow familiar because of so many dreams, he returned to sleep.

Amber couldn't remember waking so peacefully since she was a child. In fact, had she ever woken feeling this warm and snuggly, secure and happy?

There was a sound beside her, a slow, rhythmic cadence she couldn't recognise. There was a scent she couldn't define, filling every breath she took. Where was she?

Opening her eyes, she saw the light sprinkling of

dark hair scattered across an unclad male chest lying right before her eyes. She took in a slow, deep breath, and it came again, the scent of belonging, as if she'd come home at last.

She barely dared lift her gaze—but she knew the scent, the feeling it gave her. She'd known it for so long from so far away. It was him. The perfectly sculpted statue of ice had become all warm, solid male. Her untouchable husband was within her reach at last.

They had so many problems to overcome. Their hopes and fears and most of their lives were unknown to each other—but at this moment, she didn't care. He was here. She was gripped by a long-familiar urge.

Could she do it?

It had started on their wedding night when he'd come to her, dressed as a groom ready to love his bride. It had persisted even after she'd emerged from the bathroom that night, clad only in a towel. With a glance, he'd gathered his blasted paperwork and bowed to her, the movement fairly dripping with irony, and, with a twist to his lips, he'd left the room without a word. She hadn't slept in weeks after that—and she'd endured three hundred and forty-four restless, hungry, angry nights after he'd refused her bed last year. Sometimes she thought she'd give anything to have this farce come to an end, and she could find a man who would actually desire her. But he didn't, and he wouldn't let her go, either.

The *thunk* came again, a sickening hit in the stomach at the remembered rejection. So why did the aching need to taste him with her lips and tongue still fill every pore of her? Why did she want him so badly when he was so cold and uncaring? She could never seem to break this stupid desire for the husband who despised her. The need to touch him was like the heat of a gold-refiner's furnace. There was no point in ignoring facts when just by her looking at him now, by her lying so close to him, her pulse was pounding so hard she wondered if it would wake him. Wondered and hungered, as she danced on a fine blade-point of need and pride and the soul-destroying fear of another rejection.

Do it. Just kiss him once, a little voice in her head whispered, soft and insistent. *Maybe it will cure you of all this wondering. Maybe it won't be as good as you think.*

Was she leaning into him, or was she dreaming again? His lips, parted in dreams were so close, closer than they'd ever been—

His eyes opened, looking right into hers.

Her breath caught, and she danced that razor-fine point again, aching and fearful as she scrambled to find her pride, the coldness that had been her salvation in all her dealings with him. Was the returning hunger she saw in his eyes merely a product of her overwrought imagination? If only she knew him well enough to find the courage, to ask.

If only every chance she'd ever taken hadn't left her alone with her humiliation.

Harun's gaze drifted lower. Torn between slight indignation and the spark heating her blood at the slow flame in his eyes, familiar pride rushed back to save her, won over the need for the unknown. She lifted a hand to tug at the neckline of her negligée, but the other hand jerked up with it. Looking down, she saw she was tied in silken bonds, as soft as the silken negligee that barely covered her nudity beneath.

As if she had never seen him before, Amber turned back to Harun. She let her gaze take him all in. He was almost naked…and he was fully aroused.

Blushing so hard it felt like fire on her cheeks, she saw his knowing, gentle smile. He knew she wanted him, and still he didn't say a word, didn't touch her. Wouldn't give her the one thing she craved, a child of her own. Someone all her own to love.

A beautiful, almost poetic revenge for my stupid words—isn't it, Harun?—always leaving me alone? When will you stop torturing me for the past?

Taking refuge in imperiousness, she demanded, 'Who dressed me this way? Who *undressed* me? Where are we?'

His gaze lifted to hers. For a moment she saw a flash of reluctance and regret; then it vanished, leaving that unreadable look she'd come to hate. 'I'm afraid I can't answer any of those questions. I can only tell you that I didn't undress you.' He lifted his hands, tied together in front of him, with silky white bonds that would only hurt if he struggled to free himself.

Her hands were tied with the same material—and she hated that some small part of her had been hoping that he'd been the one to undress her, see her naked, touch her skin. Foolish, pathetic woman, would she never stop these ridiculous hopes and dreams? She'd always be alone. The lesson had been hammered into her skull years ago, and still she kept aiming her darts at the moon.

Feeling her blush grow hotter, she retorted, 'Well, I think I can take it for granted that you wouldn't undress me after all these years.'

His gaze roamed her body, so slow she almost felt him touch her—tender, invisible fingers exploring her skin as she'd hoped only moments before, and she had to hold in the soft sound of imagined delight. It felt so *real*.

In a deep growling voice that heated her blood,

he murmured, 'I don't think you should take that for granted at all.' After another slow perusal, her body felt gripped by fever. 'We don't have the luxury of taking anything for granted in our situation.'

Even spoken with a gentle huskiness, the final words doused the edge of her anger and her desire, leaving her soul flooding with questions. 'What's going on here, Harun? Why would anyone—anyone…just leave us here, dressed like this?'

Say it, you coward. You've been abducted! But just thinking the word left her sick and shaking with impotent terror. *So much for being like Great-grandmother…*

'I don't pretend to know.' His gaze met hers, direct. 'We just paid one hundred million dollars for Alim's safe return. How much do you think Alim and your father between them can afford to pay for our ransom now?'

'I don't know about Abbas al-Din's treasury, but the recent troubles in the Gulf have drained Father's resources, paying the security forces.' Amber bit her lip. 'Do you think the el-Shabbats are behind this?'

'I certainly wouldn't rule them out, but this could be any of a dozen high-ranking families, not just the el-Shabbats. There are many families eager to take over rulership of our countries if they only had the funds,' he said quietly. 'Your father and Alim would have to take that into consideration before making any decision.'

'Do you even think either of them knows we're gone?' she asked, hating the piteous note in her voice, pleading for reassurance.

Harun sighed. 'I don't know. Alim's got so much on his mind at the moment. We walked out saying we weren't staying. I think he'll assume we left, possibly to talk out our troubles, patch up our marriage.'

I wish we had. Why didn't you want that? she almost blurted, but there were far greater necessities to talk about right now. She looked down again, frowning. 'Why are our hands tied, but not our feet? Why aren't we gagged?'

He moved his hands, and she felt a finger caress the back of hers. 'Maybe someone wants us to talk?' he suggested, his eyes glimmering.

Her mouth opened and closed. The surprise of his making a joke was too complete for her to quite believe in it. 'Oh, I wish,' she retorted at last, rolling her eyes. 'Perhaps they could make you talk to me if they repeatedly used an electric prod—you know, those things that shock animals?'

He grinned at her, and it relaxed his austere handsomeness, making her catch her breath. 'Do you think it's worth a try?'

Choking back a giggle, she fixed a stern expression in her eyes. 'Can you please be serious? How can we get out of here?' She bit her lip.

His eyes sobered. 'I don't think they need to gag us, Amber. We're at least five storeys up. The walls are thick, and the nearest buildings are a hundred metres or more away. There are guards posted outside the doors and at every building through the windows, and they'll be very hard of hearing. I doubt that any amount of screaming will bring help.'

Absurd to feel such warmth from the motion of one of his fingers when they'd been abducted and could be dead by nightfall, but right now she'd take whatever comfort she could get. 'You've already looked?'

He nodded, his face tight. 'There's no way out of here until they let us out. This abduction's been perfectly planned.'

'Do you think anyone's looking for us yet?' she asked almost piteously, hating to hear the word. *Abduction.* It made her feel so powerless.

He gave that tiny shrug she'd always hated, but this time she sensed it was less a brush-off than an attempt to reassure her. 'That depends on how clever our abductors have been, and what they heard us saying beforehand.'

She frowned. 'What could they have heard us say?'

He just looked at her, waiting for her to remember—and after a few moments, it struck her. In her need to push Harun into action of some kind, she'd stated her intention to divorce him, where a dozen servants or any palace or government servant could have heard. She'd shown her contempt for the existing laws and traditions. Any traditional man would have been shocked.

She closed her eyes. By coming to her room to discuss their problems instead of punishing her in front of Alim, Harun had treated her with the utmost respect. But she'd given him none. She'd ploughed ahead with her shocking announcement, thinking only of humiliating Harun in a public place to spur him into some kind of action. She'd thought only of herself, her needs—and now they both had to endure the consequences.

'I'm sorry, Harun,' she whispered. 'This is all my fault.'

'Let's not waste time pushing blame at each other or on ourselves, when we don't know what's going on.' Softly, almost hypnotically, his fingers caressed hers. 'Playing that kind of game won't help either of us now. We need to keep our minds clear, and work together.'

Her head was on his shoulder before she knew she'd moved. Or maybe he had, too. Either way she rested her head halfway between his shoulder and chest, hearing him breathe, drinking it in. 'Thank you.'

'For what?'

She smiled up at him. 'A more insecure man would have wasted an hour lecturing me on my unfeminine behaviour, on my presumption in challenging you in the first place, where others could hear. A less intelligent man would blame our situation totally on me. A man who felt his masculinity challenged might have beaten me into submission.'

He smiled—no, he grinned back. 'I never even thought of it. Whatever made you think I wanted a wishy-washy kind of wife?'

In all this time, I've never seen him smile like that.

Had she seen him smile at all, apart from the practised one for the cameras?

Maybe he knew she needed distraction from this intense situation, as weird as it was terrifying; but Harun was providing distraction and reassurance in a way she never would have expected—at least from him.

Was this why his men had followed him into battle with such blind ferocity? Had he made them feel they could survive anything, too?

Whether it was real or a trick, she had no desire to argue with him. Right now, he was all she had, just as she was all he had—and the thought of losing this smiling man, teasing and caressing her hand, was unbearable. 'Well, maybe if you'd talked to me about what kind of wife you did want, I could answer that,' she replied, but in a light, fun tone, 'but right now I'm rather clueless.'

At that, he chuckled. 'Yes, you're not the only one who's told me that I keep a little too much to myself.'

Fascinated, she stared at his mouth. 'In all this time, I've never heard you laugh.'

She half expected him to make a cool retort—but instead one end of his mouth quirked higher. 'You think it took being abducted for me to show my true colours? Maybe, if you like it, you can arrange for it to happen on a regular basis.'

She was in the middle of laughter before she realised it. The look, the self-deprecating humour, set off a strange feeling low in her belly, a cross between muted terror and an inexplicable, badly timed hunger. 'How can you be so serious all the time when everything is safe and normal, and be this…this *charming* man now, when we might—?' To her horror, she couldn't go on, as a lump burned its way up her throat and tears prickled behind her eyes.

'Well, you see, I'm trying to distract myself from a horrendous itch on my back that I can't scratch.' He lifted up his bound hands.

Even though it was delivered deadpan, it made her laugh again. If he'd spent all those years before being too serious, now it seemed she couldn't make him become so. And she knew he'd done it to distract her. His thoughtfulness in this terrifying situation touched her. 'I could do it for you,' she offered, gulping away the painful lump in her throat. 'Roll over.'

He did, and her breath caught in her throat as she realised anew that he was naked from the waist up. She looked at the wealth of revealed man, unseen in three years. He didn't have time for extensive workouts, but he was toned and a natural deep brown, with broad shoulders and a muscular chest and back.

'Where?' she asked, fighting to keep the huskiness

out of her voice. It was the first time she'd touch his body, and it was for a stupid itch.

'Beneath my left shoulder blade.' He sounded odd, as if his throat was constricted, but when she scratched the area for him, using both hands at once since they were both there, he moved so her fingers covered a wider amount of skin. 'I don't remember anything ever feeling so good,' he groaned. 'You have magic hands, Amber. How about you? Is there anywhere you can't reach that needs scratching?'

Yes, my curiosity as to why you never talked to me before now, why you never wanted anything but to hurt and humiliate me until now—when we could die at any moment. 'You scratch my back and I'll scratch yours?' she murmured, aiming for the light tone of moments before, but she was too busy fighting her fingers, aching to turn the scratch into a caress, to feel his body.

'Sounds good to me,' he said, and now he was the one that sounded husky. 'I'll scratch any itch you need me to. You only need to ask, Amber.'

Her breath snagged in her chest. Her rebel eyes lifted to his face as he rolled back to her, and his awkward, tied movements brought him far closer to her than he'd ever been. His thighs were against hers, and his eyes were nearly black as his gaze slowly roamed her silk-clad form, and lifted to her mouth. She'd never seen a man's desire before, and it felt like sunlight touching her after a long, black Arctic winter. 'Harun,' she whispered, but no sound emerged from her. Her body moved towards him, and her face lifted as his lowered…

Then Harun rolled away from her, hard and fast, and she felt sick with anger and disappointment.

CHAPTER SIX

AT LEAST Amber felt sick until she realised Harun was shielding her with his body. 'Who's there?' he demanded in a hard tone. 'I heard the door open. Show yourself!' He'd blocked her effectively from seeing the door, and whoever stood there couldn't see her, either.

She tugged fast at the peignoir, but realised that trying to cover herself with this thin bit of nothing was a useless exercise.

A man walked around the curtain, his bare feet swishing on the old woven rug. He was dressed in anonymous Arabic clothing the colour of sand, most of his face swathed in a scarf. Without a word he bowed to them both, an incongruous gesture, and ridiculous in their current setting. Then, covering Amber's scantily clad body with the sheet first, his eyes trained away, he used a thin knife to untie her, and then Harun. When Harun was free the man waved to the small dining table by the window, which had two trays filled with food and drink, and bowed again.

Harun leaped to his feet the second he was untied, but the man lifted a strong hand, in clear warning against trying anything. He clapped, and two guards came around the curtains, armed with machine guns. Both guards had the weapons aiming directly at Harun.

Amber balled her hands into fists at her sides, instead of holding them to her mouth. If they knew she wanted to be sick at the sight of the weapons trained on Harun, they'd know their power over her.

If Harun felt any fear he wasn't showing it. 'What is this?' he demanded, and his voice was hard with command. 'Where are we, and what do you want with us?'

The man only kept his hand up. His eyes were blank.

'So you're a minion, paid to look anonymous,' Harun taunted. 'You can stay silent so I don't know your dialect, but the money you're hoping for will never be of use to you or your families.'

In answer, the man moved around the room. He pointed to one possible escape route after another, opening doors, lifting curtains to show them what lay beyond.

Armed guards stood at the door, and at each flat building roof facing a window, holding assault weapons trained on them.

Amber scrambled to her feet and, clutching the sheet, shrank behind Harun, who suddenly seemed far bigger than before, far more solid and welcoming. 'Those men are snipers, Harun,' she whispered. Allah help them, they were surrounded by snipers.

'Don't think about it. They're probably not even loaded,' Harun whispered in her ear. He kept his gaze on the guard, hard and unforgiving as he said aloud, 'I promise you, Amber, we'll get out of this safely.' He flicked the man a glance. 'These men know who we are. They won't take any risks with us, because we mean money. The cowards hiding behind them are obviously too scared to risk dealing with us themselves.'

The guard's eyes seemed to smile, but they held something akin to real respect. He bowed one final time, and left the room. A deep, hollow *boom* sound followed moments later.

The door wasn't simply locked. They'd put a bar across it.

Amber shivered. 'That was—unnerving.' Hardly knowing it, she reached out to him with a hand that shook slightly. Right now she was too terrified to remember it was weak to need anyone else's reassurance.

His hand found hers, and the warm clasp was filled with strength. 'It was meant to paralyse us into instant obedience,' he said, in equal quiet, but anger vibrating through each syllable. 'Remember, we're their bankroll. This is all a game to them. They won't hurt us, Amber. They need us alive.'

'So why surround us with snipers?' She shivered, drawing closer. 'Why put us in the middle of nowhere like this? How can we be such a threat?'

After a short hesitation, he took her in his arms. 'The Shabbat war,' he said quietly.

He said no more, made no reference to his heroic acts three years ago—he never had spoken about it, or referred to his title, *the beloved tiger*. But his acts were the stuff of legend now, and the stories had grown to Alexander-like proportions during the past few years. The people of Abbas al-Din felt safe with Harun as their sheikh. 'You mean they're afraid of what you'll do?'

'Thus far it seems there's nothing *to* do.' He made a sound of disgust. 'They want us to believe they're prepared for every contingency, but even the guard's silence tells me something. They don't want us to know where we are. They know if he'd spoken, I might have known his nationality and sub-tribe through the local dialect.'

She frowned, looking up at him, glad of the distraction. 'Why would you know his nationality or tribe or dialect?'

His voice darkened still further. 'Whoever took us knows that I have a background in linguistics, and that I know almost every Arabic sub-dialect.'

'Oh.' Another cold slither ran down her back, even as she wondered what he'd studied at university, and why she'd never thought to ask. 'I think I'd like to eat now.'

'Amber, wait.' He held her back by trapping her in his arms.

More unnerved by the events of the last hour than she wanted to admit, she glared at him. 'Why should I? I'm hungry.'

He said softly, 'You've been unconscious for hours, and you haven't eaten in a day. You came around the bed in fear, but your legs might not support you any further.'

So have you, she wanted to say but didn't. *I can stand alone,* her pride wanted her to state, but, again, she couldn't make herself say it, because more unexpected depths of the man she'd married were being revealed with every passing moment. And, to her chagrin, she found her legs weren't as steady as she'd believed; she swayed, and he lifted her in his arms.

'Thank you,' she whispered. It was another first for them, and the poignant irony of why he held her this way slammed into her with full force.

'Come, you should eat, and probably drink.' He seated her on one of the chairs. 'But let me go first.' This time she merely frowned at the impolite assertion. With a weary smile, he again spoke very softly. 'I don't think your body can take any more drugging, Amber. You slept hours longer than I did, and you're still shaking. Let me see if the food is all right.'

Touched again by this new display of caring for her,

Amber tried to smile at him, but no words came. Right now, she didn't know if the non-stop quivering of her body was because of the drugging, or because he was being so considerate…and so close to her, smiling at her at last. Or because—because—

'I've been abducted,' she said. She meant it to come out hard, but it was a shaky whisper. But at least she'd said it. The reality had been slammed into her with the guards' entrance. There was no point in any form of denial.

'Don't think about it.' His voice was gentle but strong. 'You need time to adjust.'

Grateful for his understanding, she nodded.

After making a small wince she didn't understand, he tried the water, swilling it around in his mouth. 'No odd taste, no reaction in my gums or stinging in the bite-cut I just made in my inner cheek. I think it's safe to drink.' He poured her a glass. 'Sip it slowly, Amber, in case it makes you nauseous.'

She stared at him, touched anew. He'd cut himself to protect her. He'd shielded her from the guard. He'd carried her to the table. The Habib Numara she'd heard so much of but had never seen was here with her, for her.

'How do you know about the effects of being drugged?' she asked after a sip, and her stomach churned. She put down the glass with a trembling hand. 'Were you a kidnapper before you were a sheikh?'

Her would-be teasing tone fell flat, but he didn't seem to care. He kept smiling and replied, 'Well, I know about dehydration, and you've been a long time without fluids. When I did a stint in the desert, it affected me far more than it should for a boy of nineteen. The next time, during the Shabbat war, I knew better.'

Curiosity overcame the nausea. She tilted her head.

'What were you doing in the desert at nineteen? Was it for the Armed Forces?'

'No.' He lifted the darker fluid out of the ice bucket and poured it in his glass. When he'd sipped at it, swilling it as he had the water before swallowing, he poured her a glass. 'I was in Yemen, at a dig for a month. There was a fantastic *tell* there that seemed as if it might hold another palace that might have dated back to the time of the Queen of Sheba. Sip the water again now, Amber. Taking a sip every thirty seconds or so will accustom your stomach to the fluid and raise your blood pressure slowly, and hopefully stop the feeling of disorientation. I'll give you some iced tea as soon as I know you can tolerate it.'

'Why were you at a dig?' she asked before she sipped at the water, just to show her determination and strength to him. She didn't want him to think she was weak because she needed his help now.

He looked surprised. 'You didn't know? I assumed your father would have told you. I studied Middle Eastern history with an emphasis on archaeology. That's why I minored in linguistics, especially ancient dialects—I wanted to be able to translate any cuneiform tablets I found, scrolls with intimate family details, or even the daily accounts.'

She blinked, taken aback. Her lips fell open as eager questions burst from her mouth. 'You can read cuneiform tablets? In what languages? Have you read any of the Gilgamesh epic in its original form, or any of the accounts of the Trojan wars?'

'Yes, I can.' His brows lifted. 'What do you know about the Gilgamesh epic?'

She lifted one shoulder in a little shrug. 'I learned a little from my tutors during my school years, and I read about it whenever it comes up in the *Gods and Graves* journal.'

It was his turn to do a double take. 'Where do you get the journals? Have you been in my room?'

She shrugged, feeling oddly shy about it. 'I'm a subscriber. I have been for years.' She hesitated before she added, 'I can't wait for it to arrive every month.'

'You know you can get it online now?' He looked oddly boyish as he asked it, his eyes alight with eagerness.

'Oh, yes, but I like to *feel* it in my hands, see the things again and again by flipping the pages—you know? And the magazine is shinier than printing it up myself. The pages last longer, through more re-reads.'

'Yes, that's why I still subscribe, too.'

They smiled at each other, like a boy and girl meeting at a party for the first time. Feeling their way on unfamiliar yet exciting ground.

'When do you find time to read them, with all you have to do?'

'Late at night, before I sleep,' he said, with the air of confession. 'I have a small night light beside the bed.'

'Me too—I don't want the servants coming in, asking if they can serve me. I just want to read in peace.'

'Exactly.' He looked years younger now, and just looking into that eager blaze of joy in his eyes sent a thrill through her. 'It's my time to be myself.'

'Me too,' she said again, amazed and so happy to find this thing in common. 'What's your favourite period of study?'

He chuckled. 'I'd love to know who the Amalekites were, where they lived, and why they disappeared.'

Mystified, she demanded, 'Who? I've never heard of them.'

'Few people have. They were a nomadic people, savage and yet leaving no records except through those they attacked. *Gods and Graves* did a series on them years ago—probably before you subscribed—and I used to try to find references to them in my years of university. I have notes in my room at home, and the series, if you'd like to read about them.'

'You'd really share your notes with me? I'd *love* to,' she added quickly, in case he changed his mind. 'Did you always want to be an archaeologist?'

He shrugged and nodded. 'I always loved learning about history, in any part of the world. Fadi planned for me to use it to help Abbas al-Din. He thought Alim and I could use our knowledge in different ways. Alim, the scientist and driver, would be the way of the future, bringing needed funds to the nation, and exploring environmentally friendly ways to use our resources rather than blindly handing contracts to oil companies. I would delve into our past and uncover its secrets. Abbas al-Din has had very little done in the way of archaeology because my great-great grandfather banned it after something was found that seemed to shame our ancestors.' He grinned then. 'When I told Fadi what I wanted to do, he gave me carte blanche on our country's past. He thought it would be good for one of the royal family to be the one to make the discoveries, and not hide any, shall we say, inconvenient finds. After the dig at Yemen, I organised one in the Mumadi Desert to the west of Sar Abbas, since Fadi didn't want me to leave the country again—but it turned out that I couldn't go.'

As he bowed his head in brief thanks for the food, and picked up a knife and fork to try the salad, she watched him with unwilling fascination. She didn't want to ruin the mood by asking why he hadn't gone that time, or why he hadn't taken it up as a career. She knew the answer: Alim's public life had chained Harun to home, helping Fadi for years. Then Fadi's death and Alim's desertion had foisted upon him more than just an unwanted wife.

He nodded at the salad, and served her a small helping. 'I think everything is okay to eat. The most likely source for drugging is in the fluids.'

After she'd given her own thanks, she couldn't help asking, 'So you keep up with it?'

'Apart from subscribing to all the magazines, I have a collection of books in my room, which I read whenever I have time. I keep up with the latest finds posted on the Net. I fund what digs I can from my private account.'

'It must be hard to love something so much, to fund all those digs you fund, and not be able to be there,' she said softly.

His face closed off for long moments, and she thought he might give her that shrug she hated. Then, slowly, he did—but it didn't feel like a brush-off. 'There's no point in wanting what you can't have, is there?'

But he did. The look of self-denial in those amazing eyes was more poignant than any complaint. She ached for him, this stranger husband who'd had to live for others for so many years. Would he ever be able to find his own life, to have time to just *be*?

As if sensing her pain and pity for him, he asked abruptly, 'So, do you have any thoughts on who might have taken us, and why?'

Wishing he hadn't diverted her yet, she bit her lip and shook her head. 'I've been thinking and thinking. This feels like the wrong time. If the el-Shabbats were going to do it, it should have been a year or more ago— and they would have paid for the African warlord to kill

Alim while they were at it. What's the point of taking us now? Alim's back, he'll probably marry the nurse… the dynasty continues.'

'I know.' He frowned hard. 'There doesn't seem to be a point—except…'

Amber found herself shivering in some weird prescience. 'Except?'

He looked up, into her eyes. 'We didn't continue the dynasty, Amber. Too many people know we've never shared a bedroom. The most traditional followers of the el-Kanar clan think you've brought me bad luck, and hate Alim's Western ways. They probably think we've already poisoned any future union, given who and what the woman is who Alim intends to marry.'

She frowned deeper. 'What do you mean, who and what she is? How could we affect his chances with this woman?'

He shrugged. 'You might as well know now. Hana, the woman Alim loves, is a nurse, and, yes, she saved his life—but though she was born in Abbas al-Din, she was raised in Western Australia, and isn't quite a traditional woman. Not only that, but Hana's not the required highborn virgin—she's a commoner, an engineer and miner's daughter. And that's not the worst.'

'There's more?' she asked, as fascinated as she was taken aback. This was sounding more and more like one of the many 'perils of Lutfiyah' films she'd enjoyed as a child.

'Believe it…or not,' he joked, in an imitation of the 'Ripley's' show she'd seen once or twice, and she laughed. 'Though Alim's arranged for her illegal proxy marriage to a drug runner to be annulled, the man's still in prison. You know how the press will use that—"our sheikh marries a drug runner's ex-wife". What's left of the Shabbat dynasty will make excellent mileage of it, perhaps start another insurrection.'

Amber gasped. 'How can Alim possibly think he'll get away with it? The hereditary sheikhs will never allow such a marriage!'

He gave another, too-careless shrug. 'Alim has brought our country much of its current wealth. And Hana's become a national heroine by saving his life at the risk of her own—without her, he'd be dead now, or he might never have come home. That belief is likely to start a backlash against the worst of the scandalmongers. And, given our lack of an heir in three years, the sheikhs that profit most from the el-Kanar family, and are desperate for the dynasty to continue, will vote for the marriage. By now Alim's probably made his planned public announcement that he either marries Hana or I remain his heir for life. To Alim, it's her or no one. He's determined to have her. He loves her.'

The bleakness of his eyes warned her not to touch the subject, but a cold finger of jealousy ran up her spine and refused to be silenced. 'She's a lucky woman. Is that how you feel about—about—what was her name?'

'Buhjah, you mean,' he supplied, with an ironic look that told her he knew she'd deliberately forgotten the woman's name. 'You really don't know me at all, Amber.'

She felt her chin lift and jut as she faced him, willing her cheeks not to blush at being caught out. 'And if I don't, whose fault is that?'

'Too many people's faults to mention, really.' He turned his face, staring out into the afternoon sky. 'And yes, the blame is mine, too—but blaming each other for anything gets us nowhere in our current position.'

'All right,' she said quietly, shamed by his honesty.

'So I'm thinking perhaps this abduction could be a reactionary thing—those who love Alim most are taking us out of the equation, or some relations of Hana's are doing this to force the media and hereditary sheikhs to accept the marriage, which means we'd be safely returned once the marriage is accepted and the wedding arrangements begun.'

She frowned at him. 'That's a very pretty story, and very reassuring, but what is it you're not saying? Who do you really think it is?'

His shoulders, which had been held tense, slumped just a little. 'Amber...'

'I'm not a child,' she said sharply. 'This is my life, Harun. I need to know what I'm facing if I'm going to be of any help to you.'

After a few moments, he came around the table and stood right over her. A quick, hard little thrill filled her at the closeness she'd so rarely known from him. 'Those who hate Alim's Western ways might have taken him, too,' he said so quietly she had to strain her ears to hear him, 'and they've put us here, in these clothes, this enforced intimacy, to create the outcome they want.'

'Which is?' she asked in a similar whisper, unwillingly fascinated. He was speaking so low she had to stand and crowd against him to hear.

'The obvious,' he murmured, moving against her as if they were playing a love-game. 'They want a legal el-Kanar heir from a suitable woman—and who could be more suitable than you?'

She felt her cheeks burning at the unprecedented intimacy. 'Oh.' She couldn't think of anything to say. But the stark look in his eyes told her something else lay deeper. 'There's something wrong with that happening, isn't there?' she mouthed against his ear. Again he didn't answer straight away, and she said, soft but fast, before she lost her courage, 'Whatever it is you fear most, just say it. It's my life, too. I deserve to know.'

The silence stretched out too long, and she wondered if she'd have to prompt him again, or make him angry enough to blurt it out, when he whispered right in her ear, 'But if we make love and you get pregnant, Amber, they'll have no reason to keep my brother alive.'

CHAPTER SEVEN

WHO was constantly conspiring against them? Even half naked and moving against each other as if they'd fall to the bed at any moment, it wasn't going to happen.

Would they ever enjoy a normal marriage, or was it Amber's pipe dream?

Then she looked into Harun's eyes, and saw the depth of his fear. *Alim is all I have left.*

An icy finger ran down her spine as she understood the nightmare he was locked in. How could she find it in her to blame him for putting his brother's life first?

Slowly, she nodded, trying to force a calm into her voice she was far from feeling—for his sake. 'Then we won't make love,' she said softly.

The intensity of his gratitude shone in the look he flashed at her. 'Thank you, Amber. I know how much you want a child. This is a sacrifice for you.'

'If it was one of my family in danger, I'd be saying the exact same thing to you.' Her voice was a touch shaky despite her best efforts. 'So tell me what's next?'

With a brief glance she didn't quite understand, he moved back to his side of the table. 'I checked the room pretty thoroughly while you slept. There's no window that isn't watched, no door or way out that isn't fully guarded, including the roof. And as you saw, there are snipers everywhere.'

'So that's it?' she asked in disbelief. 'We're stuck in this golden cage until someone pays our ransom?'

Slowly he nodded. 'Yes,' was all he said, and her stomach gave a sick lurch. Then he gave her a knowing look. It clicked into place—of course, the guards were listening in. They had to be careful what they said aloud. 'We're stuck here—and if you don't like it, remember you agreed to marry me.'

Not knowing what he wanted from her, she made herself give a delicate shrug, as if being abducted were something she was used to. 'Well, at least they're treating us better than Alim was treated in Africa.'

'And that's just as well, since Alim was always the action man in the family.'

The look in his eyes said he'd almost rather be treated badly. She frowned.

'You feel shamed by this abduction?'

He didn't look at her as he said, 'I can't get you out of this danger we're in, Amber. I searched out every possible way, but there's none that gets us both out, and in safety. I don't know what they want, but we have no choice but to comply.'

'And that makes you feel incompetent? Harun, you were drugged and brought here against your will—'

'But that didn't happen to Alim, did it? He sacrificed himself. He was even a hero in being abducted.' His jaw tightened. 'What sort of man am I if I can't even fight, or find a way for us to escape? If Alim couldn't rescue himself, what hope does someone like me have of getting us both out of here?'

The unspoken words shimmered in the air. *Even when he was taken, Alim had sacrificed himself, risked*

*his life to save the woman he loved. I am less than a
man in comparison to my brother.*

His voice rang with conviction—the kind that came
from intimate knowledge of truth of feeling. And she
wondered how many times he'd felt that way before he'd
become a hero in his own right. How hard had it been
to be the younger, quieter brother of the nation's hero,
to live in the shadow of a world superstar?

'Someone like you?' As she repeated the words an
unexpected surge of hot anger filled her, at what she
wasn't yet sure, but its very ferocity demanded she find
out. 'How did they take you?' she shot at him.

He shrugged again. It was another cool, careless
thing, a barrier in itself, and, three years too late, she
realised that this was what he did, how he pushed people away before he'd say something he might regret.
'Tell me, Harun!'

'Fine,' he growled. 'I came into the room, and saw
you being dragged away. I had no time, I just ran after
you, and they took me, too. Because I didn't stop to
think it through, I failed you. And yes, before you say
it, I know Alim would have done better!'

'*How* would he have done that?' she snapped, even
angrier now.

He shook his head. 'If I'd stopped to think—if I'd
called the guard—'

'Then they might have got away, and I'd be here
alone, terrified out of my mind.' She slammed her hand
down on the table. 'I don't *care* what Alim would have
done. He isn't here. *You're* here, because you tried to
save me. You didn't have to do that!'

'And what a wonderful job I did of it, getting drugged
myself, and ending up with us both in this prison,' he
retorted, self-mockingly.

As if incensed, she grabbed his shoulders. 'You're here with me, Harun. You think you're nothing like Alim? You're just like him! You're more of a hero to me than he can ever be. Do you think he'd have sacrificed his freedom for me the way you have? Don't you know what you did—how much it means to me?'

He looked up at her, a look she couldn't decipher in his eyes. 'You've never willingly touched me before,' he said slowly.

Lost in an odd wonder, she looked down, to where his fingers curled around her arms. 'Nor you me, before today,' she whispered. Suddenly she found it hard to breathe.

Too quickly, they both released the other, and she felt as bereft as he looked, for a bare moment in time, both breathing hard, as if from running an unseen race. It felt so real. Was it real? She only wished she knew.

'I—I'm so glad you're here with me, Harun,' she said, very quietly. 'No matter how it happened. Without you, I…' She shook her head, not sure what it was she was going to say. 'I'm glad it's *you*,' she whispered, so soft he probably couldn't hear it.

'Amber.'

So quietly spoken, that word, her name, and yet… She was torn between so many remembered humiliations and unfamiliar, almost frightening hope, her lips parted. She looked into his eyes, and saw—

The door rattled and opened.

Just as she'd looked up into his eyes like that—with a softened, almost hopeful expression, the real woman, not the part she was playing, he knew, could *feel* it— the noise of the rattling handle broke the moment. At the entry of the man swathed in his sand-hued outfit and headscarf, Amber had started, flushed scarlet and looked back down at her plate as if nothing else existed.

Harun couldn't stand up until he had control of his body—and that was a task of near-impossible proportions, given what she was almost wearing. Thus he'd desperately thought of this farce of play-acting for those watching them. If they'd known he was hurtling down the invisible highway of a man condemned to fulfilling the prophecy they'd put in place for him, they'd leave him totally alone with Amber—*your wife, she's your wife*—and she looked like the gates to paradise...

Stop it! Just don't look at her.

She wasn't looking at him like that now. In fact she wasn't looking at him at all. She waited until their guard had cleared away their food trays and left the room, before murmuring, 'Are you sure there's no way out of here? I think we should check the rooms together. There might be something...'

Pride reared its useless head for a moment, but with a struggle he subdued it. Even if he could easily take offence, he chose not to start another fight. Besides that, they both needed something to distract them right now—at least he did, and desperately.

'Good idea,' was all he could manage to say. 'I was drugged still when I looked. I might have missed something.' He knew he hadn't, but he had to get away from her.

She must have seen him stiffen. She peered at him, anxiety clear to read in her eyes. 'I just want to be sure—and, really, what else is there for us to do right now?'

He could think of something else incredible, amazing, and dangerous to do—but he nodded, trying not to look at the sweet delight before him. 'You need to know for yourself. I would have, too.'

Her voice was filled with warmth and relief. 'Thank you.'

Why wasn't it a cold evening? Then he could cover her with the bed sheet—a towel—anything. Not that it would help; the image of her unfettered loveliness had been burned in his brain since their wedding night. 'You try out here, while I do the bathroom.'

After shoving her chair back, she froze. 'I—I don't… I think I'd prefer if we stayed together. That is, if you don't mind,' she said in a very small voice. She still wasn't looking at him, but, from the fiery blush before, she was far too pale.

Harun cursed himself in silence for thinking only of himself, his needs. Amber was frightened, and he was all she had. Who else could she turn to for strength and reassurance? 'Of course I'll stay with you,' he said gently. 'Where would you prefer to begin?'

Without warning she scraped the chair back and bolted to him. 'I c-can't think. I don't know what to do.' She pushed at his shoulders in obvious intent.

Forcing compassion and tenderness to overcome every other need right now, he pushed his chair back, and pulled her onto his lap. He held her close, caressing those shining waves of dark-honey hair. 'I'm here, Amber. Whatever happens, I won't leave you.'

'Thank you,' she whispered in a shaky voice, burrowing her face into his neck. 'I'll be better in a minute. It's just that man—his silence terrifies me. And those guns…I can't stop seeing them in my mind.'

'It would scare anyone senseless,' he agreed, resting his chin on her hair. *Don't think of anything else. She needs you.*

'Were you scared? In the war, I mean?' she whispered into his neck. Her warm breath caressed his skin, and sent hot shivers of need through him. Every moment the struggle grew harder to not touch her. Just by being so close against him, she made his whole body ache with even hotter desire.

Could she feel what she was doing to him? He'd been permanently aroused since waking up the first time; his dreams had been filled with fevered visions of them that he couldn't dismiss, no matter how he tried.

For Amber's sake, control yourself. She doesn't want you, she needs reassurance.

'Of course I was scared,' he said quietly, forcing the safe rhythm, palm smoothing her hair. 'Everyone was, no matter what they say.'

'They said you showed no sign of fear.' She looked up, her eyes as bright as they'd been before, when they'd made a connection over their shared love of archaeology. It seemed his bride wanted to know about him at last. 'Everyone says you fought like a man possessed.'

Everyone says... Did that mean she'd been asking about him, or drinking in every story? What had she been thinking and hoping in those years he'd ignored her?

'I had to lead my men.' He wondered what she'd think if he told her the truth: he'd fought his own demons on that battlefield, and every man had Alim's face. Where his brother was concerned, the love and the resentment had always been so closely entwined he didn't know how to separate them—and never more so than when he discovered his bride wanted Alim. And he was paying for that ambivalence now, in spades. If Alim had been taken, or God forbid, was dead...

'Everyone said you took the lead wherever you were.' She sounded sweet, breathless.

But though something deep inside felt more than gratified that she wanted to know about him, had been thinking of him, he sobered. 'Even killing a man you perceive as your enemy has its cost for every soldier, Amber. The el-Shabbats had reason for what they did. I knew that—and Alim had left the country leaderless; he clearly wasn't interested in coming home. I wondered what I was doing when I took the mantle.'

'So why did you fight?' she murmured, her head on his shoulder now.

He wanted to shrug off the question, to freeze her out—but his personal need for space and silence had to come second now. Amber's and Alim's lives were on the line because he'd put his *feelings* before the needs of the nation. 'When the el-Shabbats chose Mahmud el-Shabbat for their leader, a man with no conscience, who was neither stable nor interested in what was best for anyone but his own family, they forced the war on me.'

'You became a hero,' she murmured, and he heard the frown in her voice. Wondering why he wasn't happy about it.

Harun felt the air in his lungs stick there. He wanted to breathe, but he had to say it first. 'I can still see the faces of the men whose lives I took, Amber,' he said jerkily. 'War isn't glorious when you live it. That's a pretty story for old men to tell to young boys. War's an undignified, angry, bloody mess.'

'I saw you coming in on the float,' she said quietly. 'I thought you looked as if you wanted to be anywhere but there.'

He almost started at her perception. 'All the glory I received on coming back felt wrong. I'd taken fathers from children, sons from parents, made widows and orphans, all to retain power that was never mine to keep.'

At that she looked up. 'That's why you gave it back to Alim without a qualm?'

Slowly, he nodded. 'That, and the fact that the power wasn't mine to give. I was only the custodian until his return.'

'You related to the people you fought against.' It wasn't a question; her eyes shimmered with understanding. Her arms were still tightly locked around his neck, and he ached to lean down an inch, to kiss her. His yearning was erotic, yes, but beneath that some small, stupid part of him still ached to know he wasn't alone. Where Amber was concerned, he was still fighting inevitability after all these years.

'To their families,' he replied, struggling against giving the uncaring shrug that always seemed to annoy her. 'I became an orphan at eight years old. I lost both my brothers almost at once.' He held back the final words, unwilling to break this tentative trust budding between them.

'And you lost your wife even before the wedding day.' She filled in the words, her voice dark with shame even as she kept her head on his shoulder. 'You were forced to fight for your family, your country while you were still grieving. You gave everything to your country and your family—then you were abandoned by Fadi, by Alim, and, last, by me. I'm sorry, Harun. You were alone. I could have, should have tried to help you more.'

How could she say those things? It was as if she stared through him to see what even he didn't. She seemed to think he was something far more special than he was. 'No, Amber. I never told you. I shut you out.' Tipping her face up to his, he tried to smile at her, to keep the connection going. 'All of it was my fault.'

'No, it wasn't, and we both know that—but blame won't help us in our current situation,' she retorted, quoting his words back to him with a cheeky light in her eyes, and her dimples quivering.

He grinned. 'Someone's feeling feisty.'

She winked. 'I told you I'd feel better in a minute. Or maybe five,' she amended, laughing.

'Then let's begin the search,' he suggested, not sure if he was relieved or resentful for the intervention. Her lips glistened like ripe pomegranates in the rose-hued rays of the falling sun through the window, and he was dying to taste them. And when she wriggled off his lap, he couldn't move for a few moments—so blinded by white-hot need for her, all he could see was the vision of them together in bed as they could have been for years now.

What sort of fool had he been? Within a day of giving her some attention her eyes were alight with desire when she looked at him, or when he was close. If he took her to bed right now, he doubted she'd even want to argue.

'Wrong time, wrong place—and Alim could die,' he muttered fiercely beneath his breath, feeling the frozen nails of fear put the coffin lid on his selfish wants.

Keeping Alim's face in his mind, Harun fell to his knees, looking for loose boards in the floor with ferocious determination. He wouldn't look at her again until his blood began to cool; but whenever he heard her husky voice announcing she still hadn't found anything, he looked up, and with every sight of her wiggling along the floor in that shimmering satin the fight began over. Hot and cold, fire and ice—Amber and Alim...

The suite of rooms was small. Amber unconsciously followed the path he'd taken while she slept, knocking softly on walls, checking bricks for secret passages. But then she hung so far out of the window he grabbed her by the waist to anchor her, and had to twist his body so she wouldn't know how much she affected him. Fighting also against the burning fury that those men with assault rifles would be looking at her luscious body, he pulled her back inside with a mumbled half-lie about her safety.

She sighed as she came back into the room. 'We're so far up, even if we tied the sheets and bedcover together, we'd have a two-storey drop or more.' She glanced at him. 'You could probably make it to the ground, but I'd probably break my legs, and then they'd just take us again.' Biting her lip, she mumbled, 'I wish I'd had the same kind of war training as you—dropping out of planes, martial arts and the like. I wish I could say I was a heroine like my great-grandmother, but the thought of breaking my legs makes me sick with fear.' She looked him in the eyes as she said, 'You should go without me. You have to save Alim.'

Hearing the self-sacrifice in her voice, remembering how she'd been so furious when he'd run himself down earlier, even if it was an act, he felt something warm spread across him. After all these years where he'd ignored her, did she really think so much of him?

Or so little, that she could even suggest he'd go without her, put his brother first, and abandon her to her captors?

Quietly, he said, 'I dropped out of planes with a parachute and spare. And even if I could use a sheet as a makeshift parachute, and jump in the darkest part of the night, I'd still have to outrun the guards, and find a place of safety or a phone, and all without water or food—and wearing only these stupid things.' And there was no way he'd leave Amber alone to face the consequences of his escape.

He was taken aback by the success of his diversion when Amber giggled. 'Oh, the visions I'm having now—the oh-so-serious Sheikh Harun el-Kanar escaping abduction, but found only in his boxer shorts!'

Though he laughed with her—because it was a funny thought—right now he wasn't in the mood to laugh. 'I would never leave you, Amber. That probably seems hard to believe—'

Her eyes, glowing with life and joy, a smile filled with gratitude, stopped him. She did believe him, though he'd done nothing to earn her trust. That smile pierced him in places he didn't want to remember existed. The places he'd thought had died years ago…trust, faith, and that blasted, unconquerable hope.

Trust had died even before his parents, and, though he still prayed, a lot of his faith had eroded through the years. And hope—the last shards of it had smashed to bits when he'd heard her agree to marry him, despite loving his brother.

Or so he'd thought, until today.

'Let's check the bathroom again,' she suggested. 'Sometimes there's a loose tile on the floor that is the way out—or even in the bath itself. My great-grandmother had one egress made through the base of the tap in the bath, after the war ended. We should check it out thoroughly.'

Grateful for the reprieve from his dark thoughts, he followed her in and got down on hands and knees beside her, but turned to search in the opposite direction.

Anything rather than endure the torture of memory—or of watching her lovely body wiggling with every movement.

This time he forced his eyes to stay away. If she held a shadow of desire for him now, it was just through enforced proximity and her need for human closeness. She'd never shown a single sign of wanting him, or even wanting to know him better, until now. He'd never seen anything from her but cold duty and contemptuous anger until the day she'd heard Alim was back.

That was the way his life would be. How many times did he have to convince himself over and over that duty and supporting family was his only destiny? How many times had his parents told him that he'd be useless for anything else? How many times in the twenty-two years since they'd died had Fadi enforced his belief that duty was first, last and everything for him, that he was born to be the supportive brother? Yet here he was, no wiser. At thirty years old, he still hadn't learned the lesson.

Was it the after-effects of the drugs that had weakened his resolve, or was it just a case of too many years of denial? But the desire in her eyes, the curve of her smile, the music of her laughter—and everything that was almost clear to see beneath that peignoir—were killing him to resist. Even the sight of her bare feet was a temptation beyond him right now.

This was the exact reason he'd avoided her so long before. But now he couldn't make himself avoid her, even if he could parachute out of here with that stupid sheet. He couldn't leave her alone…and so here they were, only the two of them and that delicious bed… and with every moment that passed, it became more impossible to resist her. How long could he last before he made a fool of himself?

But that was exactly what the kidnappers wanted, and damned if he'd give it to them.

CHAPTER EIGHT

By NIGHTFALL, they had covered almost every inch of both rooms, and found no way out. All her hopes dashed, she sat on the ground, slumping against the cool bath tiles in despair. 'We're not getting out of here, are we?'

'Not until they let us out.' There was a strange inflection in his voice.

Arrested, she turned to look at him. 'What is it?'

Harun didn't reply.

'I'm not a child, Harun, or an idiot. I'm in this with you, like it or not, and there's nowhere for you to conveniently disappear to here, no excuse or official or quiet room for you to get away from me. So you might as well share what you're thinking with me.'

After a moment that seemed to last a full minute, he said, 'I think your father may be our abductor.'

'What?' They were the last words she'd expected. Gasping, she choked on her breath and got lost in a coughing fit to be able to breathe again. Harun began using the heel of his hand in rhythmic upward motions, and the choking feeling subsided. Then she pushed him away, glaring at him. 'Why would he do that? What would be the benefit to him, and to Araba Numara?

How could you even think that? How dare you accuse my father of this?'

Harun was on his haunches in front of her, his face had that cold, withdrawn look she hated.

'For a daughter who doesn't share my suspicions, a daughter who believes implicitly in her father's innocence, I notice you put the two most natural questions last. Instead, you asked the most important questions first—why, and what benefit to him in abducting his own child. You believe it's possible at the very least, Amber. Everything makes sense with that one answer. Why there have been no demands or threats as yet, why we were left in this kind of room dressed this way, and why we're alone most of the time. Your father has probably endured some ridicule and speculation over our not producing an heir, and he wants it to end.' He gave her a hard look. 'He has no son, and you're the eldest daughter. He hasn't named his brother, or his nephews or male cousins as his heir. Any son we have will be qualified to become the hereditary sheikh for Araba Numara, so long as he takes his grandfather's name...and I assume that keeping the line going is important to him.'

Every suspicion he'd voiced could be exactly right. And it all fitted her father too well. Though he came from a very small state in the Emirates—or maybe because of that—he enjoyed manipulating people until they bent to his will. And yes, he'd want a grandson to take his name and the rule of Araba Numara.

'If you're right, and I'm not saying you are, I will never, never forgive him for this.' Then she shot to her feet, and cried, 'Hasn't he done enough to me? Three years of being his pawn, left in a foreign country and shuffled from one man to another, none of whom wanted me! Can't he just leave me be?'

The echoes of her voice in the tiled bathroom were her only answer. The silence was complete, just as it had always been when she'd tried to defy her father's will, and she slid back down the tiles. 'I hate this, I hate it. Why can't he let me have my life?'

Harun's eyes gleamed with sadness. 'I don't know, Amber. I'm no expert on family life. I barely remember my father, or mother.' As he slid down beside her, the feeling of abandonment fled along with her outrage—and, as natural as if she'd done it for years, she laid her head on his shoulder. 'It's probably best not to think about it,' he said quietly, wrapping his arm over her shoulder, drawing her closer. 'And remember I could be wrong.'

'We both know you're not. It makes too much sense.'

'There is the other solution I told you before,' he said very quietly.

She nodded.

'If they won't let us out until you're pregnant, we may have little choice but to comply.'

A tiny frisson of shock ran through her. 'B-but what if we are wrong—wouldn't that risk Alim's life?' she stammered.

'Only if he has been taken. We just don't know.' His eyes hardened. 'I can't keep living my life for honour alone, Amber. Alim's the one who left his family and his nation too many times to count—and why did he finally return? For the sake of a woman he can't even marry. I've done everything for him for ten years, and it's time I did something I want to do.'

Softly, she murmured, 'And now you want me?'

'Yes,' he replied, just as soft.

His mouth curved; his eyes softened. And he brushed his mouth against hers.

With the first touch, it was as if he'd pulled a string inside her, releasing warmth and joy and need and—and yes, a power she hadn't known existed, the power of being a woman with her man, *the* man for her. She made a smothered sound and moved into him as her lips moved of their own will, craving more. She turned into him, her hands seeking his skin, pulling him against her. Eager fingers wound into his hair, splayed across his back, explored his shoulders and arms, and the kiss grew deeper and deeper. They slowly fell back until they lay entangled on the floor. Amber barely noticed its cold hard surface. Harun was touching her at last, he was fully aroused, and she moaned in joy.

'As far as first kisses go, that was fairly sensational,' he said in a shaky voice. 'But we're only a few hours out of the drugs. Today hasn't been the easiest for either of us. Maybe we should rest. If we feel the same tomorrow...'

Bewildered by the constant changes in his conversation, she sighed. 'Yes, I think I need to sleep again. But I really should have a bath.'

After a short silence, Harun said quietly, 'No, sleep first. Come, I'll help you to bed.' He swept her up again, as though she weighed nothing, and carried her back out to the main room. He could have taken her to bed and made love to her all night and she'd have loved it.

Reaching the bed, he laid her down. 'Rest now, Amber. I swear I won't leave you,' he whispered, his voice tender, so protective. Had the *habib numara* become her very own tiger—at least for now?

She ought to know better than to think this way. They barely knew each other, and he'd never shown any interest in touching her until today.

She ought to feel grateful to their abductors. For

the first time Harun was looking at her as a person. For a captive, she felt happier than she had in a very long time.

Too tired to work through the confusion, she allowed her heavy eyes and hurting heart to dictate to her. She needed temporary oblivion from the events of the past day, to blank it all out. But even as she slid towards sleep, she felt Harun's presence in the chair he'd drawn up beside the bed. Touched that he was standing guard over her, keeping her safe without presuming to share the bed, she wanted to take his hand in hers and cradle it against her face, to thank him for all he'd done today. But he'd done so much for her; she couldn't demand more than he'd already given. She sighed again, and drifted into dreams.

And shaken far beyond anything she knew, too aroused to sleep, Harun sat beside her the whole night. He didn't get on the bed—he didn't dare—but he remained on guard, ready to protect her if there should be a need.

She's a stubborn, rebellious daughter, with no regard for law or tradition. I wouldn't pay a single dinar for her return. Let Sheikh el-Kanar pay it, if he's worried about her at all, but I doubt it. He ran from her in the first place, didn't he?

Shivering in the night suddenly turned cold, the echoes of her father's uncaring tone still ringing in her ears, Amber jerked to a sitting position in the bed. Praise Allah, it had only been a nightmare—

But this bed, sagging slightly, definitely wasn't hers, and choppy breathing came from a few feet away. Adjusting to the darkness and unfamiliar room, she gradually took in the form of her husband sleeping in a chair beside the bed.

Although the sight of him made her ache somehow—he looked like a bronze statue of male perfection in the pale moonlight, even half crumpled in the chair—reality returned to her in seconds, the reasons why they were here. And what they'd done to convince their abductors that they were cooperating...

A hot shiver ran down her spine.

She looked again at her sleeping husband, realising anew the masculine beauty of him. His face was gentle in repose, seeming so much younger.

She reached out, touching him very softly. His skin was cool to the touch. He was shivering as she'd been; there were goosebumps on his arms. His sheet must have slipped to the floor long ago, and he was still half naked, only clad in those silky boxers. Obviously he'd left her the blanket, but she'd kicked it off some time in the night.

During the search earlier, neither of them had found a second covering of any kind, so she could do nothing but share the blanket they had. The modesty he'd given her in sleeping on the chair was touching, but it was ridiculous when they were married. If either of them took sick, they had no way to care for the other.

'Harun,' she whispered, but he didn't move. Taking him by the shoulder, she shook it, feeling the flex and ripple of muscles beneath her fingers. 'Harun, come—' she stopped herself from saying *come to bed* only just in time '—under the blanket. You're cold.'

An indistinct mumble was his only response.

Impatient, getting sleepy again, she grabbed his shoulders with both hands, pulling him towards her.

'Come on, Harun. You'll be in agony in the morning, sleeping like that. I can't afford for you to get sick.'

Something must have penetrated, for he fell onto the bed, landing almost right on top of her, his leg and arm falling over her body, trapping her. 'Mmm, Amber, lovely Amber,' he mumbled, moving his aroused body against hers, his lips nuzzling her throat. 'Taste so good…knew you would. Like sandalwood honey.' And before she could gather her wits or move, he kept right on going, lower, until he was kissing her shoulder, and she had no idea if he was awake or seducing her in his dreams.

She couldn't think enough to care…her neck and shoulder arched with a volition of their own as he nibbled the juncture between both, and the bliss was *exquisite*. And when his hand covered her breast, caressing her taut nipple, the joy was sharp as a blade, a beautiful piercing of her entire being. 'Harun, oh,' she cried aloud, craving more—

His eyes opened, and even in the moonlit night she saw the lust and sleepy confusion. Gazing down, he saw his hand covering her breast. 'I'm sorry…I was dreaming. I didn't mean to take advantage of you.' He shook his head. 'How did I get on the bed?'

A dull ache smothered the lovely desire like a fire-retardant blanket. 'I woke up—you were shivering, and I pulled you over. The sheet wasn't warm enough for you,' she replied drearily. Who had he been dreaming of when he'd said her name? 'It's all right. Take the blanket and go back to sleep.'

'Amber…'

'Don't,' she said sharply. *Don't be kind to me, or I*

might just break down. She rolled away from him so he wouldn't see her humiliation. 'Goodnight.'

The next afternoon

Any moment now, he'd pick her up and throw her on the bed, and make love to her until they both died of exhaustion.

He'd been going crazy since last night. Pretending to sleep for her sake, he'd lain still on the bed until his entire body had throbbed and hurt; he knew she was doing the same. Then, just as his burning body talked him into rolling over and making love to her, her soft, even breathing told him she slept.

That he'd made Amber cry simply by not continuing to make love to her was a revelation to him. In three long, dreary years, all he'd known was her contempt and anger, even the night she'd asked him to come to her bed. But within the space of a day, he'd seen her show him regret, budding friendship, trust, need and—for that blazing second when he'd awoken with his hand on her breast—pure desire for him. He'd come so close to giving in, giving them what they both wanted—only a tiny sound from outside the room, a shuffle of feet, a little cough, had reminded him of their watchers, had held him back.

And how could he risk his brother's life?

It kept going back to that choice: their personal happiness, or Alim's life. If there was a way to know Alim was safe, if they could escape and have some privacy, he'd give their abductors what they wanted, over and over. Now he knew Amber wanted him…

But without meaning to, he'd hurt and humiliated

her. His apology had wounded her pride in a way she was going to find extremely hard to forgive.

After hours of silence between them and no touching, he spoke with gentle deliberation. 'I'm sorry about last night.'

Her lips parted as her head turned. 'You already apologised. Anyway why should you apologise? You were dreaming, right?' Oh, so cold, so imperious, her tone—but his deepest male instincts told him it was the exact opposite of what she felt inside.

He looked into her eyes. 'I heard a cough outside the room. The first time I make love to you will not be by accident, with an audience of strangers through holes in the wall.'

A surprised blink covered a moment's softness in her eyes. 'That's a fairly big assumption to make.'

Despite the cold fury in her voice, he wanted to smile. 'That we'll make love? Or that you can forgive me for neglecting you all these years, and welcome me in your bed?'

'Either. Both,' she said quietly, 'especially considering the neglect was of epic proportions, and publicly humiliating.'

At that, he offered her a wry smile. 'I had no wish for a martyr bride, Amber. I'm fairly sure you didn't want a dutiful, reluctant husband, either. I believed you had no desire for me; you believed that I never desired you. All this time we both wanted the same thing, if only we'd tried to talk.'

She looked right into his face, her chin lifted. 'Did you really just say that—if *we'd* tried to talk?'

He had to concede that point if he wanted to get anywhere with her. 'You're right, I'm the one that didn't

try—but ask yourself how hard you'd have tried, if you'd
thought I was in love with your sister.'

Another slow blink as she thought about it. 'Maybe—'

But just as the frost covering her hidden passion finally began to soften he heard the door open, and he
cursed the constant interferences between them—but
then, with a smothered gasp, Amber bolted off the window seat and cannoned into him. 'He's pointing that
rifle at me,' she whispered, shaking, as his arms came
around her. 'And…and he's looking at me, and I'm only
wearing this thing.'

Like a whip he flung around to face the guard, putting Amber behind him. 'What is this?' he demanded
four times over, in different dialects. 'Answer me, why
do you terrify my wife this way?' Again he said it in
another few dialects—all of Amber's home region.

The man never so much as glanced their way; he answered only by moving the rifle inward, towards the
dining table.

Amber's chest heaved against his back as she tried
to control her fear.

Three men followed him into the room, bearing a
more substantial meal than they'd eaten yesterday, or
at breakfast, three full choices of meal plus teas, juice
or water. The men set the table with exquisite care, as
if he and Amber were honoured guests at a six-star
hotel. Then they held out the seats, playing the perfect waiters—only the maître d' was holding an assault rifle on them.

Harun stood his ground, shielding Amber with his
body. 'Move away from the chairs. Don't come near
my wife. Stop looking at her or I will find who you are
after this and kill you with my bare hands.'

After a moment, with a look of deep respect the head

guard bowed, and waved the others back. When they were out, he took several steps back himself before he stopped, staring at the furthest wall from their captives.

Harun led Amber to her chair and seated her himself, blocking her from their view so they could see no part of her semi-exposed body. 'Now get out,' he barked.

He bowed again, and left the room.

'Thank you,' she whispered, hanging onto his hand when he would have moved.

'There's nothing to thank me for.' Some emotion he couldn't define was coursing through him, as if he were flying with his own wings. He didn't trust it.

'I can't take much more of this—this terrifying silence,' she muttered, her free hand clenching and unclenching. 'Why did he point the rifle at me? What did I do?'

Harun had his own ideas, but he doubted saying, *Their objective is achieved, Amber, you ran straight to me,* would help now, or bring her any comfort. She might even begin to suspect him.

Instead of sitting, he released her hand, and wrapped his arms around her from behind. 'I know I may not seem like much help to you in this situation, Amber, but I swear I'll protect you with my life if need be.'

She twisted around so her face tilted up to his. 'You know that's not true. Last night, I told you how glad I am you're here…and you saw, you must have seen that…' Her lips pushed hard together.

It was time; he knew it, could feel it; but still he would give her a gift first. 'Yes, I saw that you desire me, how you loved my touch.' With a gentle smile, he touched her burning face. 'And you had to see how much I desire you, Amber. If it hadn't been for the guards, we'd have made love last night.'

She said nothing, but her eyes spoke encyclopaedic volumes of doubt. 'You said my name. I wasn't sure if you meant it.'

In the half-question, and the deep shadows in her eyes, he saw the depth of the damage he'd done to her by his neglect. She had no idea at all; she'd never once seen his desire until last night, and she even doubted it had been for her.

It seemed he'd hidden his feelings too well—and at this point he doubted just showing her would be enough. He had to open up, starting now.

'I did mean it, Amber. My dreams were of you. My dreams have been of you for a long time.' Taking her hand again, he lifted it to his mouth and pressed a lingering kiss to her palm. When she didn't snatch her hand away, but drew in a quick, slightly trembling breath, he let his lips roam to her wrist. 'Sandalwood honey,' he murmured against her skin. 'The most exquisite taste I've known.'

She didn't answer him, except in the tips of her fingers that caressed his face, then retreated. So tentative still, she was afraid to give anything away. Unsure if, even now, he'd walk away again and leave her humiliated. He'd damaged her that much through the years, which meant he had the *power* to hurt her—and that meant more than any clumsy words of reassurance she could give.

It was time to give back, to be the one to reach out and risk rejection.

So hard to start, but he'd already done that; and now, to his surprise, the words flowed more easily. 'You need to know now. I haven't been with any woman since we married. I kept my vows, as difficult as that's been at times.'

Her look of doubt grew, but she said nothing.

He smiled at her. 'It's true, Amber. I didn't want a replacement. I wanted you.'

The little frown between her brows deepened. 'Then why…?'

Walking around to face her, he took both hands in his and lifted her to her feet. 'I refused to continue last night because our audience made it clear they were there watching us. I'm not a man who likes applause and cheering on, and I didn't think you'd want your first time to be here, where any of them could see us.'

'No, I wouldn't. Thank you for thinking of it,' she murmured, her gaze dropping to his mouth, and his whole body heated with a burst of flame at the look in her eyes. 'But I don't understand why you didn't come to me before—oh.' She nodded slowly. 'Because of what I said to my father.'

'I'm not Alim. I'll never be like Alim.' She had to know that now. He'd rather burn like this the rest of his life than be his brother's replacement in her eyes, or in her bed.

'I know who you are.' And still she stared at his mouth with open yearning that made him define the alien, flying feeling—he was so *glad* to be alive, to be the man she desired.

Then her head tilted, and he mentally prepared himself: she did that when she wanted to know something he wouldn't want to answer. 'Why do you think you can never compare to Alim? I barely knew him. You must have known that; he left for the racing circuit days after I met him, and then ran from the country as soon as he could leave the hopspital. He never wanted me, and you say you did. So why didn't you try for me?'

As far as hard questions went, that was number one.

He felt himself tensing, ready to give the shrug that was his defence mechanism, to walk away—

Trouble was, there was nowhere to go, no place of escape. And he knew what she was going to say before she said, very softly, 'You promised to talk to me.'

At that moment he almost loathed her. He'd never broken a promise in his life, never walked away in dishonour; but trying to put his disjointed thoughts together was like trying to catch grains of sand in a desert storm. What did she want him to say?

'Just tell me the truth,' she said, just as quietly as before, smiling at him. As if she'd seen his inner turbulence and wanted to calm it.

Nothing would do that. There was no way out this time. So he said it, hard and fast. 'I don't compare to him. I never have. What was the point in trying for you when you wanted a man that wasn't me? I was never anything but a replacement for him, with Fadi and with you. I always knew that.'

CHAPTER NINE

I<small>F THERE</small> was anything she'd expected Harun to say, it wasn't that. She'd hoped to hear a complaint about his family, or about how he'd lived in the shadow of a famous, heroic brother—but never that calmly spoken announcement, like a fact long accepted. *I don't compare to him. I never have.*

A sense of foreboding touched Amber's heart, a premonition of the hardships facing her if she chose to spend her life with this man. *How would I have ended up, had Alim been my brother, if I'd lived in the shadow of a famous sibling and ended up taking on all the responsibilities he didn't want?*

The thought came from deep inside her, from the girl who'd never really felt like a princess, but a commodity for sale to the highest bidder. And she spoke before she knew what she wanted to say. 'That's another big assumption to make, considering my total acquaintance with Alim has been five days, and I've known you three years.'

He flicked her another resentful glance, but she wouldn't back down. He had nowhere to go, and his honour meant more than anything. He'd answer her, if she waited long enough.

Lucky she wasn't holding her breath; she'd be dead

by the time he finally said, 'I know what I am in your eyes, Amber. And I know what Alim is.'

She frowned. 'One sentence made in grief and not even knowing you, and that's it? You just write me off your things to do list? *Marry her and ignore her because she insulted me once when she didn't know I was listening? I don't care if she apologised.*'

Another look, fuming and filled with frustration; how he hated to talk. But finally he said, 'I'm not Alim.'

By now she felt almost as angry as him, but some instinct told her he was deliberately pushing her there to make her stop talking to him. So she'd keep control if it killed her. 'That sounds like a statement someone else told you that you're repeating. And don't tell me Fadi ever said it to you. He adored you.' After a long stretch of silence, she said it for him. 'How old were you the first time your parents told you that Alim was better than you?'

The one-shoulder shrug came, but she didn't let herself care. So he said it, again with that quiet acceptance. 'I don't remember a time when they didn't say it.'

He wasn't angry, fighting or drowning in self-pity. He believed it, and that was all.

Bam. Like that she felt the whack of a hammer, snatching her breath, thickening her throat and making her eyes sting. His own parents had done that to him? No wonder he couldn't believe in her; he didn't know how to believe in himself. And the truth that she'd pushed away for years whispered to her inside her mind, why she'd fought to push him out of his isolation and to notice her. *I love him.*

Every messed-up, silent, heroic, inch of him. He'd crept into her soul from the time he'd marched away with his men, and returned a hero, hating the adulation.

She'd been amazed when he'd handed everything back to Alim without wanting a thing. She'd thought him so humble. Now she knew the truth: he didn't think he deserved the adoration of the nation; that was Alim's portion. He'd been in the shadows so long he found the limelight terrifying.

Don't you see, Amber, I'm doing everything I can do?

The words he'd given her in rejection of creating a child with her finally made horrible sense...and she knew if she pushed him to tell her everything, he'd never forgive her.

'Before our wedding, my father told me that the lion draws obvious admiration, but you need to look deeper to see the tiger's quiet strength. I've known that was true for a long time now,' she said softly, and touched his face. Warm and soft, not the unyielding granite she'd found repellent and fascinating at once; he was a man, just a damaged, honourable, limping, beloved hero, and she loved him.

He stared at her, looked hard and dazed at once. He shook his head, and her hand fell—but she refused to leave it like that. She touched him again. *'Habib numara,'* she whispered. 'I've wanted you for so long.'

He kept staring at her as if she were a spirit come to torture him—yes, she could see that was exactly what he was thinking. He needed time to believe even in this small miracle. So she smiled at him, letting her desire show without shame or regret.

After a long time, he took her by the hands. *'Mee johara,'* he said huskily. *My jewel.*

Her heart almost burst with the words, pounding with a joy she'd never known.

Don't hesitate, or he'll think the worst. So she wound her arms around his neck. 'I've been alone so long, waiting for you,' she whispered so softly only he would hear it. 'Kiss me and call me your jewel again.'

But instead, the hard bewilderment filled his eyes again. 'You've waited for me?'

'So long,' she murmured against his ear, and let her lips move against his skin. She felt him shudder, and rejoiced in it. 'You fascinate me with the way you can make me hate you and want you and love you—'

He stilled. Completely. And though she waited, he didn't ask her if she meant it. She felt his pain radiating from him, the complete denial of what she'd said because he didn't dare believe, not yet. Lost in a life of expectation and self-denial, in a world where his own parents didn't seem to love him, at least in comparison to Alim, how could he believe?

In a life where both of them had hidden their true selves from self-protection, one of them had to step into the light…and at least she'd known her family loved her. For once, she was the strong one; she had to lead the way.

'I love you, Harun. I have for a long time.' She pulled back, her hands framing his face as she smiled with all the love she felt. 'It began when I saw you march away to war, and I kept wondering if I'd see you again. I heard all the stories of your courage, leadership and self-sacrifice, and was so proud to be your woman. And when you came back and refused to talk about it, but just kept working to help your people, I began to believe I'd found my mate for life.'

His frown grew deeper with every word she said. 'Before we married.' The question was hidden inside the incredulous statement. He didn't believe her.

With difficulty, Amber reined in her temper and said, 'I never looked at you before we were engaged—

but once we were, I couldn't stop looking at you. But on our wedding night, I thought you didn't want me at all. I thought you hated me. I was only nineteen, I was told nothing but to follow your lead…I didn't know what to do.'

At last his features softened a little. 'So you followed my lead, all these years.'

She murmured, 'Pretending to despise you when all I wanted was to be in your life, in your bed. I cried myself to sleep that night.' Inwardly her pride was rebelling more with every word she spoke, but the relief at finally getting the words out was greater. Besides, pride wouldn't help either of them in this situation. Neither would useless worry over who heard their conversation—given the people they were, that would happen no matter their location. 'If I'd known why you avoided me…'

He moved an inch closer, his features taut with expectation, and she exulted in the evidence that he wanted her. 'What would you have done?'

'This,' she whispered, and kissed him.

It was a clumsy attempt, a bare fastening of her lips on his, and she made a frustrated sound. She felt his lips curve in a little smile as he put his hands to her hips and drew her closer, and took over, deepening the kiss, arousing her with lips and hands until she forgot everything but him.

Let your husband show you the way. For years she'd felt nothing but contempt for her mother's advice—it had only led her to utter loneliness and self-hate. But now Harun showed her the way, and the joy spread through her like quicksilver. He had one hand in her hair, another caressing her waist while he kissed her, and she found her body taking over her will. She moaned and kissed him even deeper, moving against him and the fire grew. Oh, she loved his touch, the feel of his body sliding on hers—

Were they in bed? She didn't remember moving her feet, or landing on the mattress; his hand was on her breast again and it was that knife-blade touch of exquisite perfection...

Then there was only the soft swish of air on her skin, and she made a mewing sound of protest before she could stop it. 'Harun?' she faltered, seeing him standing beside the bed. 'Did I do something wrong...?'

'No...something very right.' He finished pulling the curtains around the bed, and turned to smile at her. 'It will only be wrong if you tell me you want to stop.'

The black blankness was gone from his eyes; the ugly memory had been chased away, and by her. She felt her mouth curving; her eyes must be alight with the happiness and desire consuming her. 'After waiting three years for you, do you think I could?' No matter who was there, or why they'd come to this place, or what happened in the past, they were here now. He was all hers at last. 'Now, Harun. Please.'

And she held out her arms to him.

CHAPTER TEN

The next morning

So THIS was what she'd waited so long to know...

Through the cracks in the curtains he'd pulled around the bed last night, the rising sun touched Harun's sleeping face; his breathing was soft and even. Slowly Amber stretched, feeling a slight soreness inside her, but what they'd shared had been worth every discomfort.

He'd been right. With each touch, each kiss and intimate caress, the feeling went from wonderful to exquisite to an almost unbearable white light of beauty, until the ache inside her, the waiting and the wanting was intolerable, and she thrashed against him in wordless demand. And still he kept going, teasing her in kiss and touch until she'd pleaded with him to stop the sweet torture, and take her.

She was so ready for him that the pain was brief, a cry and a moment's stiffening, and it was done; soon the ache was to know the joy again. She kissed him and moved her body so he moved inside her. He smiled and called her his jewel again, and the familiar endearment, one her parents had given her years ago, was so much more beautiful from his lips, with his body on hers, inside her.

They made love slowly, Harun giving her infinite tenderness and patience. The beauty built higher as she became ready for the next step, and he took her there. The joy became bliss, and then something like being scorched by the sun, and yet she couldn't care, couldn't fear it or want to stop. And just before she cried out with joyful completion, he whispered, 'I can't wait any more—Amber, Amber...'

He shuddered in climax almost at the same time she did. As he held her afterwards, he caressed her hair and whispered, *'Mee habiba `arusa.' My beloved bride.*

She smiled and refused to give in to the temptation to ask if he meant it. The whispers in the women's rooms the past few years told her that men could become tender, poetic even at these times, but could forget it in minutes.

They made love twice more in the night, once at her instigation. If she was awake, she couldn't stop herself from touching him or kissing him.

Looking at him laying beside her now, his face almost boyish in sleep, his brown skin aglow in the light of sunrise, she felt her body begin the slow, heady tingling of arousal. Leaning into him, she kissed his chest, loving the taste of his skin. Unbearable to think of stopping now—she kissed him over and over, in warm, moist trails across his body.

His eyes were open now, and he was smiling at her. Her insides did that little flip at the relaxed, happy man who was finally her lover, and she was lost in wanting him. 'Come here,' he growled, and pulled her on top of him.

Laughing breathlessly, she whispered, 'I'm sorry I woke you.'

Now the smile was a grin. 'No, you're not.'

She bit her lip over a smile. Was she a fool to feel so happy? Did she care? 'No, I suppose I'm not sorry at all.'

'So this is how it's going to be, is it? I'll be worn out by your constant demands?' His twinkling eyes told her how much he hated the thought.

'I'm sure you knew I was a little on the demanding side when you married me,' she retorted, mock-haughty, but she moaned as his lips found better uses than teasing.

This time he taught her new things that pleased him, and she let him know what she loved, and it was beyond beauty, more than physical bliss. It was joy and peace. It was deep connection, communication without words. It was happiness so complete she couldn't think of anything to match it.

She'd heard about the endless pleasure of making love, but never had she dreamed this act of creation could be so life-changing. It was far from just her body's gratification; it was giving a part of herself, her trust, her inner self to Harun, and he gave himself to her.

She wondered if he felt the same, or whether it was this way every time he—

No, she wouldn't think of his former lovers now. She couldn't bear to think of him in this intimate position with another woman. She was his lover now, and he was hers. And she'd make sure it stayed that way.

'Are you in pain at all?' he asked as he held her afterwards.

'A little,' she admitted.

'Stay there a minute.' He got out of bed, and walked into the bathroom, wonderfully naked, and she couldn't help staring at his body. Unable to believe that, because of an abduction of all things, she finally had him all to herself. And within two days, they'd become lovers.

Had the passion been there all along, simmering beneath the surface? What might have happened long ago had he not overheard her silly girl's romantic dream of marrying a superstar? If she hadn't overreacted to his coldness on their wedding night—a decision she knew now he'd made in a mixture of intense grief and betrayal—would they always have had this joy together?

The sound of running water was soon followed by a lovely scent, and she smiled when he came back into the room. Then the mere sight of him, unclad and open to her in a way he'd never been, made her insides go all mushy with longing. 'Come.' He lifted her into his arms with ease. How had she been so blind, never realising until now just how big and strong he was?

He placed her in the bath, which was hotter than she normally liked it, and she squealed, and squirmed. 'The heat will help with the discomfort,' he said, his voice filled with tenderness. 'The bath oils can be good for that, too, I've heard. Just wait a few minutes.'

Deciding to trust him in this, she settled into the water with a luxurious wriggle, and soon she discovered he was right; the soreness lessened. 'Thank you, this is really helping,' she said as he came back into the room with the bed sheet. 'What are you—?' She stopped as he began washing it at the sink. 'Oh…thank you.' She blushed that he'd do something so intimate for her, and not think it beneath his masculine dignity.

He turned his face and smiled at her. 'What happened is nobody's business but ours. It's a hot day, so it should be dry by tonight. Besides, you need time to recover.'

She'd wondered what their kidnappers would make of the bloodstain on the sheets—or even the sheet hanging out of the window to dry; but his thoughtfulness touched her anew, even as his unashamed nakedness, and just his smile, made her insides melt. 'Are you sure about that?' she murmured huskily.

He made a sound halfway between laughter and a groan. 'You're going to kill me, woman. I need time to recover.'

'Oh. I didn't know men had to recover,' she said, rather forlornly. 'I just thought you might like to share my bath…there's plenty of room, and it's so lovely and warm…'

The sheet was abandoned before she finished the thought, and he was in the enormous, two-person bath with her, hauling her onto his lap. 'Recovery be damned. You're definitely going to kill me, Amber el-Kanar my wife,' he muttered between kisses growing hotter by the moment, 'but at this moment, I can't think of a better way to go.'

As she dissolved under his touch neither could she.

The next day

It was only as they finished breakfast that the conversation of the first night began working its way up Harun's consciousness from the dazed mist of contentment and arousal he'd been happily wandering in. The guards no longer intruded on them, but knocked on the door and left food there. They waited in silence at either end of the corridor, not moving or speaking. The assault rifles were no longer trained on them from the windows.

'How much longer do you think they'll keep us here?' Amber asked, as lazily content as he.

He didn't want to break their bubble by saying *when they know you're pregnant*. And then Alim was in real danger. 'So you're tired of my company already?' he teased.

Predictably, she blushed but smiled, too. 'Not quite yet.' As if to negate the words, the underlying fear they'd both been ignoring—that if their abduction wasn't the work of her father, the danger was still real and terrifying—she came around the table and snuggled into his lap, winding her arms around his neck. After a long, drugging kiss, she whispered, 'No, not quite yet—but this has got to be the strangest honeymoon two people ever had.'

He smiled up into her face, so vivid with life, flushed with passion. 'That's a bad assertion to make to a historian, my bride.'

'I love stories about history,' she murmured, nibbling his lips.

Between kisses, he mumbled, 'In the Middle Ages, a honeymoon was a very different thing from what it is now. A man who wanted a woman—or if he needed her wealth, dowry or the political connections she brought, but couldn't have her by conventional means—drugged her, kidnapped her and constantly seduced her. He did so by keeping her half drunk on mead—that's a honeybased wine—for a month, until the next full moon, so her father would know she'd been very properly deflowered. Then he'd bring her back to her family, with the woman hopefully pregnant, and present the father with the fait accompli. If the father didn't kill him, but accepted the marriage, he'd then ask for the dowry, or the hereditary title and lands, or whatever it was he'd wanted.'

'So what's different from this situation?' she demanded, smiling, with more nibbling kisses. 'Okay, we didn't have the wine, but we had the political marriage, the drugs, the abduction, and the deflowering.'

'True,' he conceded the point, deepening the kiss before saying, 'but I assure you I didn't organise this, I didn't drug you, and I have no further demands for your father. I'm perfectly happy with what I have right now.' *Apart from not knowing whether my brother is alive or dead...*

Her eyes seemed to be always alight now, either with teasing or with passion. 'I'm enough for you, then?'

More than enough—you're everything I've ever wanted, he thought but didn't say. They were lovers now, but he had no idea where they'd go from here. She wanted him, she'd even said she loved him; but he couldn't begin to believe she wanted more from him than this time. Proximity, passion, fear, curiosity—to end her three-year shame, or to have the baby she'd demanded from him a year ago. Whatever the reason she'd given herself to him, he didn't know. Since they'd made love, neither of them had spoken beyond the here and now.

The only thing he knew for certain was that they must get out of here, and soon. Their private time here was running out, and the only emotion he could bring up was regret. Could they keep up their amity, their passion, when the world intruded on them once again?

'I should have thought of this plan myself, years ago,' he said, grinning and kissed her to distract himself from his dark thoughts. 'We could have been doing this for years.'

'Who says it would have worked on me then?' she demanded, mock-haughty but with twinkling eyes, and he laughed and showed her how easily it would have worked with a touch that made her moan in pleasure.

'Tell me more historical titbits,' she muttered between kisses growing more frantic by the moment. 'I love the way you teach me about history.'

He didn't know if she meant it or not, but he began telling her of ancient marriage rituals in their region, while she kept murmuring, 'Mmm, that's so fascinating, tell me more,' between explorations of his body with her hands, fingers and lips.

They soon returned to bed, whispering historical facts to each other in a way they'd never been intended.

'I want to please you, *mee numara,*' she whispered as she caressed his body with eager innocence. 'Show me how your—how to make you happy.'

How your other women touched you. He heard what she'd left unspoken, but again he barely believed she could be jealous. 'You please me constantly already.' Surely she could see that in the way he couldn't stop touching her?

A fierce look was his answer. 'So you won't return to her.' It wasn't a question or a plea, but a demand. She wanted him all to herself—she did care—and some deep core of ice he'd never known existed inside him began to melt.

Caring for him made this her business now; it was time to tell her the truth.

'You have nothing to fear, Amber. You never did,' he said in a jerking voice because telling anyone someone else's secret wasn't in his nature. 'You know Buhjah means joy. It was Fadi's nickname for Rafa, the woman he loved, and she loved to hear it again when Fadi was gone, from the other person closest to him. Naima is Fadi's daughter, my niece. I've never touched Buhjah; I see her as my sister-in-law. In fact I arranged a very advantageous marriage for her a few months ago, and, though part of her still loves Fadi, she's very happy.'

Amber's mouth fell open, and her eyes came alight. 'Do you mean that? There is no other woman?'

The ice inside him was melting so quickly it unnerved him, but she'd been open with him, and deserved the whole truth. 'There never has been. I've never knowingly broken a promise in my life. I wasn't going to start with our marriage vows.' He saw the look in her eyes; he had to stop her, because she was about the say the words he couldn't yet believe in, and he wasn't sure he wanted to hear them. So he grinned and said, 'So long as you're in my bed, I'm content. Even if there were fifty other women in the room right now, you leave me too exhausted to think of looking at them.' Exhausted, sated and so incredibly joyous: how could she be worried? She was a demanding and giving lover beyond any he'd known.

Her face, her whole body glowed with a furious kind of intent he'd never seen until he touched her, his warrior woman. 'No other woman but me.' Again, it wasn't a question; she was demanding her rights with him. No other woman had ever demanded so much of him, but her fierce, unashamed possessiveness made him come as vividly alive as she. In making love, Amber had none of that cold, queenly pride, but a ferocious need for him, an attitude of *'you're mine'* that translated in every touch, throbbed in every word, and made him feel so glad to be her lover. 'While you're in my bed, I don't want to look at another woman,' he vowed solemnly.

With an inarticulate little cry she leaped at him, and with a kiss he took them both beyond thought.

They spent the afternoon in bed. Not that there was much else to do, but he thought now it wouldn't matter

if there was a choice; their need for each other was almost blinding. Once in a while he wondered who was
listening or watching, but then she'd touch or kiss him,
and they were gone again.

Later that night, contented once more, Amber
wrapped herself in the sheet to use the bathroom, and
trod on the bed curtain, pulling it down. Scrambling
behind the ones still hanging in place, and making sure
she was covered by the sheet, she whispered, 'Fix it,
Harun, quickly!'

Loving that she could be so demanding and unin-
hibited with him and yet was so modest otherwise, he
rolled off the bed. Then he felt himself being jerked
back down to the bed with a thump. Half indignant, half
laughing, he was about to kiss her when she shook her
head, and her mouth moved to his ear. 'Harun, I think
I know how we can escape.' She laid her hand across
his lips. 'Put the curtains back in place, but leave the
end with me.'

The imperative command spoken beneath her breath
put his brain back in order. He hung the cheesecloth
back in its place. He'd just turned to her when she put
a finger to her lips. He nodded, and crawled across
the bed to reach her. 'Make sounds as if we're making
love,' she mouthed.

Puzzled but willing to indulge her, he made a soft
groaning sound, and another, and bounced, making the
old bed squeak, and he heard the soft swishing of feet
moving from the holes in the wall. The guards had obviously been ordered to give them privacy.

She nodded and waved her hand. *Do it again.*

As he continued she folded the end of the curtain
over, and looked closely. She probed it with her fingers.
Pulling something from the bedside table, he couldn't

make out what in the darkness, she moved it into the material. Then she whispered in his ear, 'This is one of the hairpins they gave me. If we twist them a bit, we can use them like clothing pins. We can use a curtain each, doubled over, and weave the pins through to hold the edges together.'

'You're going to make us wear togas?' he whispered back, trying hard not to laugh, but intrigued nevertheless. He made another necessary noise.

She nodded, her face adorably naughty in response to his groan. 'We girls played dress-ups enough as children. I destroyed sheets and curtains regularly until the servants complained, and Father made materials available to me. I made my sisters be my emperors or slaves. I was always Agrippina or Claudia, of course.' And then her grin faded. 'And the rest of the curtains we can tie together with the sheets.'

The simple brilliance of the plan caught him by surprise, as did her knowledge of Roman empresses' names. *She really does love history.* 'In the middle of the night, I take it?'

She nodded again. 'You go first, since you have the greatest chance of making it safely down, while I make, ah, appropriate sounds.' She nudged him, and he groaned again, while she sighed and moaned his name. 'Then I follow.'

He shook his head. 'No, you'll go first.' The slowest person had to go first. Then if anyone saw them, or the light came early or a check, he could jump down and—

'No,' she whispered urgently. 'You weigh more than me, and these curtains might not last long. I'm not athletic, and I might panic if the curtains begin to give. If you're already down...'

'I could catch you,' he whispered back, seeing the sense in that.

'You can get away,' she finished at the same time. 'You're the important one—you have to live. I couldn't bear it if you were hurt, or caught because I let you down.' Then she moaned again. 'Oh, my love, yes…'

Words she'd said while making love, but he'd taken them with a grain of salt in his experience, women became very affectionate during the act when he pleased them, and he'd never had a more compatible lover than Amber.

But she'd said it now: *My love*…and it disturbed him somehow, left him with that restless, needing to get out of here feeling. Yet she was willing to sacrifice herself—she saw him as the important one—and it caught him like a jab to the solar plexus. He'd always been the replacement, with the disposable life. Until now. Until Amber.

Did she really mean it? The doubts were insidious, but part of him now, a part so intrinsic he wouldn't know how to get them out of his system.

'Amber,' he groaned, and then whispered, 'I'll go first, but only because I can catch you—and because you're more vocal than me, during, ah…'

With a grin, she jabbed him in the side with her elbow, and he chuckled low. *Objective achieved,* he thought with a wry twist to his lips. She was distracted—and more, she was laughing. It was stupid, but he wanted her to stay happy for what would probably be their last day together. He could see her plan working. Already he was adding to her plan, with his commander's training—and planning what to do when he had Amber safe somewhere. If his brother had been taken, or, Allah forbid, killed, he knew what he had to do. If Alim was safe, the plan barely changed.

Though he had no choice but to go ahead with finding their abductors, he could no longer conjure up anger, humiliation or regret. In this abduction, he'd been given a gift beyond price. He could barely believe Amber had been in front of him for years and he'd been too angry, too betrayed or just too plain stupid to look for the passion beneath her ice when she looked at him, and her courage under this extreme test.

But for now, he had to go forward. If she was still willing when he'd found their traitors… 'So we do this tonight. We can go home.'

A few seconds too long passed before she answered. 'Yes. Um, wonderful.'

He looked at her, frowning, and saw the uncertainty he heard in her voice mirrored in her forlorn expression. 'This is your plan, Amber. Why are you hesitating?'

Still wrapped only in the sheet, she wiggled her toes, and shook her head. 'It's silly.'

'I can't agree or disagree with that statement until I know what "it" is,' he said, concerned. Though it was hard to see her expression clearly in the waxing moonlight to the east, he thought she looked lost. After a while, she gave a little half-shrug—and with a small start, he realised it was an unconscious emulation of his own act when he wanted to hide his emotions. 'Tell me, Amber.'

'You'll think I'm stupid,' she muttered. 'You'll laugh at me.'

So Amber really cared what he thought about her. Touched, he took her hands in his. 'No, I won't, no matter what. I promise. Now tell me.'

She couldn't look at him; her hands pulled out of

his as she looked anywhere but at him. Frowning, he watched her, and waited.

After a few moments she spoke, her voice low, but clearly fumbling for words. 'Out there—' her arm shot out, her finger pointing towards the window '—everything will change; we won't be able to control what happens. You'll have duty—your responsibilities, or your work, or maybe at last you can do whatever you want to do with your life. I don't know what I'll have.' She lifted her face, and she was so beautiful and so sad he wanted to haul her close, kiss her and tell her it would be all right; the world, their families and life wouldn't come between them. But he couldn't guarantee anything at this point, and she knew it.

'I ruined your plans, didn't I? I never thought beyond here and now, or what you wanted.' He tipped her face up to his. 'Did you want your freedom so badly?'

An almost violent shake of her head answered him. 'I regret nothing. You—you've made me so happy, if only for a few days.' Her hair fell over her face. She seemed very small and fragile. 'I don't know what to do now. I don't know what's in my future. It's different for you, the whole world's there for you, anything you want, but what do I do, Harun? Where do I go from here?'

An ache filled him, not for his sake but hers. Raised only to be a sheikh's wife, to be a political helpmate and child-bearer, Amber had now lost her chance to be another man's wife, to bear children. From what Aziz had told him, the only career she'd been trained for was that of a powerful man's virgin bride, his consort and mother of his children. If she'd been taught to believe it was her only use, no wonder she was lost now. 'I can't answer those questions. Only you can do that.'

Her head shook almost violently. 'I can't. I'm not—I'm not ready.'

'You're not ready for what?'

'To leave, to give up, to go back to—to the life I had before. I don't want to go back to that…that emptiness. I've been so happy here.' She looked up again, and in the time between sunset and moonrise he still saw a look of sadness so profound, the ache grew and spread through his body.

The irony didn't escape him. It had only taken being abducted to show him how little palace life meant to Amber. He felt awful, having left her alone in it so long; but how could he have dreamed the imperious princess who'd cried at the thought of marrying him could be so happy here, in a place with few creature comforts, and being alone with him? With just a small amount of his attention she'd become the most giving, ferocious, amazing lover he'd ever known.

He was happy now with what they had, so happy, but she was lost. He wanted to help her, but at this moment he didn't know what she needed most—his reassurance or her freedom. 'What can I do to help?'

She leaned forward and whispered harshly, 'We could die tonight.'

'Yes,' he agreed quietly, wondering where she was going.

She shuffled her feet on the bed, twisting her hands around each other for a few more moments, and finally whispered, 'I'm not ready to let you go, Harun. I need you one more time before the world comes between us.'

He almost let out a shout of laughter, an exclamation of amazement and the pure joy of it, but, remembering his promise, he held it in. 'That's all you want?'

She gave a tiny headshake. 'It's all I'm asking for

now…no decisions to make, no family to please, no duty to perform, no anger or pride or servants' gossip. Just give me tonight.' Dropping the sheet, she burrowed her body against his, burying her face in his neck. 'Just give me you, one more time.'

Shaking, his arms held her tight against him. How had he ever been so stupid as to believe he'd married a cold wife? By heaven, this woman was a warm-hearted, generous miracle, a gift from God who'd given him chance after chance every time he'd screwed it up or hurt her again. But this time he wasn't going to leave her crying, alone with her pain, leaving her to hide behind her only solace, her pride.

He laid her tenderly back on the bed, and closed all the window shutters and the bed curtains before returning to her. 'Just you and me.'

Her lips fell apart, and her eyes glowed. 'Thank you,' she breathed, as if he'd offered her a treasure beyond price.

'You're welcome.' Was his voice as unsteady as it sounded to him? After three long, lonely years, he realised what he could have had with Amber all along: a willing wife and lover as generous as he could have dreamed, a woman who didn't care in the least about his family name or position; all she wanted was him.

Give me a chance. It's all I'm asking.

It was all she'd ever asked of him: to give her a chance to show him the woman she really was inside. But he'd just kept pushing her away until he'd been given no choice in the matter. The chance she'd asked for had been forced on him, and he'd only given her grudging trust. Their alliance had been years too late, forged from desperation. And still, when he thought of what Amber had given him in return…

Praise God for their abductors, and this ruthless method of bringing them together.

How could he let her go after this? Was this the last night he'd ever have with her?

'You can have whatever you want. Just ask and it's yours, I swear it,' he said, even now only half believing she'd take him up on it.

Her eyes shimmered at his words. 'Do you think, when we go back, we could maybe go on a honeymoon? Just us, you and me?'

Something inside him felt as if it burst open, something tightly locked away too long. 'Of course we can. I'll have a few things to do first, but as soon as they're done...'

She nodded, and kissed him. 'Of course. I can wait.'

She'll wait for me. He smiled, and wondered if he'd ever stop smiling again. 'We know we don't need to take the honey-wine with us.'

'No, and you don't need to drug me.' Her returned smile was a thing of pure beauty. 'You'll ravish me day and night, and I'll let you.'

'I'll do my poor best.' He bowed as he laughed. 'Let me? I doubt you'd let me stop, my jewel. And you'll ravish me.'

'Of course I will,' she replied earnestly, as if he'd asked her for reassurance.

In all his life, he'd never remembered feeling like this—as if he could fly. The hope he'd believed dead was back, the terrible, treacherous thing he hardly dared to believe in was whispering to him that, this time, he wouldn't be hurt or left alone; he'd finally found the one who would want to stay with him. 'I have a yacht off Kusadasi on the Adriatic Sea. I haven't used her in years. We could cruise through the Greek Islands, or we can head to the east if you prefer. It'll be just you and me, for however long you want.'

'Oh, Harun…' She wound her arms around his neck, and buried her face in his shoulder. He heard her mumble some words, but, though he couldn't make them out, he felt the warmth of her tears against his skin, and then her lips roaming him in eager need.

Squelching that traitor's voice inside him, knowing he had to leave her first, he lifted her face and kissed her.

CHAPTER ELEVEN

How long do I want with you? I want for ever.

Had he heard her say it? She didn't know. All she knew was that in the last few days, she'd truly become a woman—and the frustrated desire she'd known for so long, the admiration and longing for her husband had become total and utter love without her even noticing. Harun had ignored her, but he'd never intentionally hurt her; he'd left her alone, but he'd fought for peace in Abbas al-Din, and worked himself half to death to hand his brother a country in good economic and political shape when Alim returned.

Had Alim ever really been a champion in her eyes? Perhaps in a public way, but it was nothing in comparison with the way she saw Harun.

During the past three years, Harun had shown her the real meaning of the word *hero*. Being a hero didn't have to come in flashy shows or trophies or spilling champagne in front of cameras; it wasn't in finding wealth, writing songs or poetry or giving flowers; it was in wordless self-sacrifice, doing the right thing even when it hurt, giving protection and—and just giving, expecting nothing in return.

She loved the man he was, and she no longer needed or even wanted fancy words or riotous acclaim. She just needed him, her quiet, beloved tiger, her lover and her man, and now she had him to herself, she never wanted to let him go again.

But she knew there was little choice in that. She'd lose him again; but for now, she'd take what she could with him.

'What do you want most to get from your job?' she asked while they waited for the deepest part of the night.

He didn't ask her to explain; he knew what she wanted: to connect with him, to know him. 'It's the really ancient history that fascinates me—our early ancestors. The Moabites during the Ishmaelite period, and Canaan, with the Philistines to the west. I want to know who they were beyond the child sacrifices and the multiplicity of gods.'

She held in the shudder. 'They sacrificed children?'

'Yes, they sacrificed their firstborn to the god Malcam, believing it brought his blessing to their crops. Archaeologists have found the sites of newborn cemeteries all over modern-day Israel and Lebanon, Jordan and Syria.'

This time she couldn't hold it in. 'That's disgusting.'

'Our ancestors weren't the most civilised people.' He grinned. 'But what I want most of all is to discover traces of the real people called the Amalekites. It's still hotly contested by historians as to who they were, because they just seemed to disappear from the human record about three thousand years ago.'

'How can that be?' she asked, wide-eyed. 'How can a whole nation of people just vanish without trace?'

'They didn't—there are records, but none belonging to them. It seems they were a warrior-nation that didn't keep their own records. Other contemporary nations speak of them as the most terrifying warriors of their time…oh, sorry, I must be boring you to sleep,' he teased as she tried valiantly to hold in her third yawn.

'No, no, I want to know,' she mumbled, snuggling deeper against his chest. 'I'm listening, I promise—just sleepy.'

Harun smiled down at her, and stroked her hair as she fell into a deep sleep. He could give her an hour; it was just past midnight.

It was heading for two a.m. when he woke her.

Instinctively Amber reacted to the gentle shaking by rolling into him, seeking his mouth. It was amazing how quickly she'd become accustomed to needing him there. 'I'm sorry, I let you sleep as long as I could,' he whispered, after they'd shared a brief, sweet kiss. 'We have to start on the plan.'

With difficulty, she reoriented herself. 'Of course, I have the pins ready. We'll need to be as silent as possible.'

'If we make any noise, I'll make some lover-noises to cover it, and you do that laughing thing you do.'

She felt her cheeks heating, but smiled. 'I can do that. Now help me pull the curtains down. We'll just take one down at a time—and while I'm making one toga, check the windows to see how many guards are stationed.'

The curtains proved no hardship in pulling off the rail, except in the slight swish and slide of falling off the rail, once it was loosened. She pulled him to her and deftly wound the doubled fabric over his shoulder and around his waist. 'What I wouldn't give to be able to rip the towels into strips,' she murmured as she had to push the pin-head through the fabric every time. 'Then we could have a waist-sash.'

He groaned her name softly, and pushed the bed

down with his hand. If they got quiet for any length of time, the guards would return. 'Here, let me.' He twisted the ends of the pushed-through pin so each end bent back on itself. 'No chance of its undoing now. Put one at my waist and it should be fine.'

'Two is better.' She worked two pins into the waist, at the rib and hip level. 'Now if one goes the other will hold.'

They both made appropriate noises while he got down another curtain and she made her toga; he helped her twist the pins, and the cheesecloth felt surprisingly strong under his hands. Amber felt breakable in comparison, or maybe it was the fear in her eyes.

They continued making sounds of love as he twisted the remaining curtains and sheets together in sailing knots.

It was time. It was nearly three a.m. and they couldn't keep up the noises much longer, or the guards would become suspicious. Seeing the fear growing in her eyes, he held her hands, smiled and whispered, 'You know what to do. I'll pull the rope three times when I reach the bottom. Be strong, my Kahlidah, my Agrippina.'

She gulped at the reference to her great-grandmother. 'I'm trying, but right now I don't think I take after her.'

She was falling apart at the worst possible time, and he had only seconds to pull her back together. 'I'm relying on you, *mee numara,* my courageous tigress. This is your plan. You can fulfil it. You *will* do this.' And he kissed her, quick and fierce.

'I think I'll leave any roaring until later,' she whispered with a wavering smile.

Harun winked at her. 'I'll be waiting for you.'

With one swift, serious look he kissed her a final time; with a little frown and eyes enormous with fear and strangely uncertain determination, she waved him off.

He crept to the window, and checked as best he could. If guards were posted around he couldn't see them—but then, he thought the numbers of guards had thinned out in the past day. They'd achieved their first objective, he supposed, and would let them enjoy their faux honeymoon.

At first, he had thought that with every piece of furniture but the chairs being nailed to the floor, he could use a bigger piece as a ballast. The closest to a window least likely to attract attention was the dining table—but now it looked too old, fragile; it might break under his weight. After scanning the room again, he saw the only real choice was the bed, since the wardrobe was too wide, taking rope length they couldn't afford.

The bed was the furthest from any window. This was going to be tight.

He looked at her again, and pulled at each corner of the bed, testing its strength, while Amber covered the noises as best she could with cries of passion, but her eyes were wide and caught between taut fear and held-in laughter.

The sturdiest part of the bed was the corner furthest from the window, but he estimated that would leave their rope at least eight feet short. Having jumped from walls in his army training, he knew they couldn't afford the noise he'd make in landing, or in catching her. If she'd come that far, seeing the gap.

This was Hobson's choice. A swift prayer thrown to heaven, and he made his decision, tying the rope with a triple winding around the nearest bed leg and through the corner where the mattress rested.

Then, slowly and with the utmost care, he let the

makeshift rope out of the window closest to the bed, and in the middle of the room, an inch at a time. It was frustrating, wasting time they didn't have, but throwing the rope could lead to its hitting something and causing attention.

At last the rope could go no further. He leaned out, and saw the rope was only short by about three feet, and he breathed a quiet sigh of relief, giving Amber a thumbs-up.

Her smile in the moonlight was radiant with the same relief he felt. With a short, jaunty wave and another wink hc hoped she could see, he climbed over the sill, gripped the cheesecloth in both hands and began the drop.

The hardest part was not being able to bounce off the building, but just use his hands to slide down. By the time he'd reached the smoother sheet part of the rope, his hands were raw and starting to bleed. He and Amber had discussed this even as they'd loved each other the final time; she knew what to expect.

He only hoped her courage saw her through. But she was only twenty-two—what had he done with life by then? Yes, he'd passed all his training exercises with the armed forces, but that was at the insistence first of his parents and then Fadi. He'd replaced Alim and Fadi at necessary functions, but again, he'd been trained for it all his life. He'd told Amber how to rappel down the rope, but if she panicked—

In his worry over her, he'd rappelled automatically down the final fifty feet. His toga was askew, but his pins held. Running even by night in their bare feet would bc hard, harder on Amber; would they make it?

Stop thinking. He looked around and again saw no guards. Vaguely uneasy, he checked out their surroundings, and tugged on the rope slowly three times. Within moments he saw her looking out of the window. Beckoning to her lest she back out, he hoped he'd done enough.

It was long moments before she moved—time they didn't have; the eastern sky was beginning to lighten. Then she slipped over the edge and, using only her hands, began dropping towards him. His heart torn between melting at her bravery and pounding with fear that she'd fall, he braced himself to catch her.

She stopped at the point where the sheets took over from the curtains, and he almost felt the raw pain her hands were in. He did feel it; his hands took fire again, as if in sympathy.

Come on, Amber. I'm waiting for you...

A few moments later, she began sliding down—literally sliding—and his heart jack-knifed straight into his mouth.

Allah help me!

A slight thump, and a madly grinning Amber was beside him, looking intensely proud of herself. 'You thought I was falling, didn't you?'

He wanted to growl so badly the need clawed around his belly, but instead he found himself kissing her, ferocious and in terrified relief. 'Let's go.'

'Which way?'

He pointed. 'I can't believe I didn't recognise where we were before, but from above the perspective changes, I suppose. This was one of the first battle areas during the el-Shabbat war. We're only about fourteen miles from Sar Abbas.'

Her face changed, losing some confidence. 'Fourteen miles. I can do that,' she whispered, frowning like a child facing a wall. 'Let's run.'

His uneasiness growing—why wasn't anyone trying to stop them?—he took her hand and ran southwest. Towards the dimly lit road only a mile away where he hadn't been able to see it before, behind the part of the building without windows. The brighter lights of Sar Abbas glinted in the distance like a welcoming beacon.

CHAPTER TWELVE

The Sheikh's Palace, Sar Abbas, a few hours later

IN THE opulent office that had been Harun's but was now his, Alim stared at Harun when he walked in the door unannounced, and then ran headlong for him. 'Praise Allah, you're back, you're alive! *Akh, mee habib akh!*'

Brother, my beloved brother. Harun had the strangest sense of déjà vu with Alim's outburst, the echo of words he himself had spoken only a few weeks ago in Africa. But Alim sounded so overwhelmingly relieved, and Alim's arms were gripping his shoulders hard enough to hurt. He didn't know what to make of it. 'So you were given demands?'

'No.' His brother's face was dark with stress and exhaustion as they all sat down on respective chairs around his—*Alim's* desk. 'This never went public, but two guards were found drugged in the palace the night you disappeared, and another almost died saving me from an abduction attempt. I came to check on you and you were gone—and Amber too. We sent all our usual guards away, and filled the palace with elite marine guards. Under the guise of army exercises I've had the best in the country looking for you, and hunting down your abductors. How did you get away? What happened?'

'I wish I knew.' Harun frowned. 'It was like they wanted us to get away. The guards disappeared, and we rappelled down a rope of sheets and curtains. We ran to the highway into the city and I called in a favour from an army captain who drove us the rest of the way.' He grinned. 'We only stopped to change, since our attire wasn't quite up to palace standards.' He flicked the grin over to Amber, who was watching him with a look of mingled pride and exasperation—at his cut-down version of events, he supposed.

'Maybe their plan was contingent on us all being taken,' Alim said quietly. 'Any thoughts on that, *akh?* You're the tactician in the family.'

'He's more than that,' Amber interjected sharply, the first words she'd spoken.

'Alim didn't mean anything by it, Amber.' He reached over, touched her hand to quiet the protest he felt wasn't yet done.

'I meant it as a compliment, actually, Amber.' Alim was frowning. 'Harun's the one that saved the country while I was lying in a bed in Switzerland, and he ran the country while I drove a truck.' He met Harun's eyes with an odd mix of admiration and resentment. 'I've only been here a few days and I've got no idea how you did it all so well.'

Harun felt Amber gearing up for another comment born of exhaustion and—it made him want to smile— the urge to protect him, and he pressed her hand this time. 'We think it might have been some el-Kanar supporters who wanted an heir.'

'You mean they wanted an heir from you and Amber?' At his nod, he earned a sharp look from Alim.

'And who don't support my, shall we say, less than traditional ways, and my choice of bride.' When Harun didn't answer, he was forced to go on. 'Then I can assume the rumours about the state of your marriage were correct?'

Neither moved nor spoke in answer.

After a flicked glance at them both, Alim avoided the obvious question. Amber's face was rosy, her eyes downcast. It was obvious she was no longer the ice maiden she'd seemed to be the week before…and Harun could almost swear Alim's left eye drooped in a wink. He certainly seemed a little brighter than before.

'So I'd guess you think the plan was to kill me and install you as permanent ruler.'

It wasn't a question, but still Harun nodded and shrugged. 'That's what they planned, but they left one thing out of the equation.' He met his brother's enquiring look with a hard expression. 'I never wanted the position in the first place. I still don't want it. Stepping into Fadi's dead shoes was the last thing I wanted three years ago. Less still do I want to be in your shoes now.'

Alim stilled, staring at him. 'You don't want to be here at all, do you.'

Again, it was a statement of fact.

'He never did.' Amber spoke with the quiet venom of stored anger. 'Tell him, Harun. Tell him the truth about what you've sacrificed the last thirteen years so he could do whatever he wanted.'

Alim only said, almost pleading, *'Akh?'*

'Amber, please,' Harun said quietly, turning only his head. 'I appreciate what you're trying to do, but this is not the time.'

'If not now, when…?' Then Amber's eyes swivelled to meet his, and she paled beyond her state of exhaustion. 'You're going to sacrifice yourself again—you'll sacrifice us, even—to fulfil your sacred duty. And for *him.*' She jerked her head in Alim's direction. 'Is he *still* all you've got?'

'Harun?' Alim's voice sounded uncertain.

Harun couldn't answer either of them. He was lost in the humbling knowledge that she could read him so easily now—that he had no time to formulate an explanation; she knew it all. And she wasn't going to support him.

When he didn't speak Amber made a choking sound, and turned on Alim. There was no trace of her old crush as she snarled at his brother, 'You'll let him do it for you again, won't you? Just as you let him do everything *you* were supposed to do, all these years. He gave up *everything* for you, while you were off playing the superstar, or feeling sorry for yourself in Africa, playing the hero again. Did you ever *care* about what he wanted? Did you think to ask him, even once?'

In the aftermath of Amber's outburst, all that was audible in this soundproof room was her harsh breathing. She stared at Alim in cold accusation; Alim's gaze was on Harun, tortured by guilt. Then Amber turned to him, her eyes challenging. She wasn't backing down, wasn't going to let him smooth this over with pretty half-truths.

The trouble was, his mind had gone totally blank. It had been so long since anyone asked him for unvarnished truth or stripped his feelings bare as she'd just done, she'd left him with nothing to say.

At length she turned back on Alim. 'Harun never told me any of it, just so you know. Fadi did. I hope you've appreciated your life, because Harun gave it to you! And he's going to do it again. For once, Alim, be a real man instead of a shiny image!'

Then, pulling her hand from Harun's, she turned and ran from the room.

Harun watched her go, completely beyond words. Devastated and betrayed, she was still loyal to him to the end. Why was it only now that he realised how loyal she'd always been to him?

Loyalty, courage and duty…Amber epitomised all of them, and he'd never deserved it.

'Have you hated me all these years?' asked Alim.

The low question made him turn back. Alim's eyes were black, tortured with guilt. 'Don't,' he said wearily when Harun was about to deny it. 'Don't be polite, don't be the perfect sheikh or the perfect brother, just this once. Answer me honestly. Have you hated me for having the life I wanted at your expense?'

For years he'd waited for Alim to see what he'd done, to ask. For years he'd borne the chains that should have been his brother's—and yet, now the question was finally asked, he couldn't feel the weight any more. 'I hated that you never asked me what I wanted.' Then he frowned. 'What do you mean, the perfect brother?'

Alim pulled a face of obvious pain, and rubbed at the scars on his neck and cheek. 'I need some of Hana's balsam,' he muttered. 'Don't pretend you don't know what I mean. It was always you with Fadi—Harun this and that, you did such a wonderful job of something I should have done or been there to do. Even if I'd come home, I'd have done a second-rate job. I was always well aware you were the one Fadi wanted, and I was second-best.'

It was funny how the old adage about walking in another's shoes always seemed so fresh and new when you were the ones in the shoes. 'I never knew he did that.'

Alim shrugged, retreating into silence, and it looked

like a mirror of his own actions. So it meant that much to Alim. It had hurt him that much.

He'd just never realised they were so alike.

'It must have hurt,' he said eventually, when it was obvious Alim wasn't going to speak. This was new to him, being forced to reach out.

Another shrug as his brother's face hardened and he rubbed at the scarring. Though it wasn't quite the same, it was a defence mechanism he recognised. He thought Amber would, too…and she'd have tried again from a different position. Poking and prodding at the wound until he was forced to lance it.

Suddenly Harun wanted to smile. All the things he'd been blind to for so long… Amber knew him so well. How, he didn't know. She must have studied him at a distance—or maybe it was just destiny. Or love.

That the word even came to him with such clarity shocked him. What did it mean?

'Do you know what it's like to be inadequate beside your little brother at your mother's funeral?' Alim suddenly burst out. 'Fadi never let me forget it. No matter what I achieved or did, I never measured up to you.'

Harun stared at him. '*Fadi* said that?'

'All the time,' Alim snarled.

It was hard to get his head around it: the brother he'd always adored and looked up to had played favourites, just as their mother and father had. The insight turned all his lifelong beliefs on their heads—and the indestructible Racing Sheikh became a man like any other, his big brother who was lost and hurting.

The trouble was he didn't have a clue what to do with the knowledge that the brother he'd resented so long was the only one who could understand how it felt to be him. 'Did you hate me for that?' he faltered.

A weary half-shake, half-nod was his only answer, yet he understood. 'I'm sorry, Alim,' he said awkwardly in the end, but he wasn't sure what he was apologising for.

Alim gave another careless shrug, but he saw straight through it. Some scars bled only when pulled open. Others just kept bleeding.

'So, what did you want to do with your life that you didn't get to do, while I was off being rich and famous?' Alim tried to snap, but it came out with a humorous bent somehow.

Willing them both to get past what had only hurt them all these years, Harun grinned. 'Come on, *akh*. I don't change. Think. Remember.'

Alim frowned, looking at him with quizzical eyes... and slowly they lit. 'The books, the history you always had your nose stuck in as a kid? Do you want to be a professor?'

'Close.' The grin grew. 'Archaeologist.'

'Really?' Alim laughed. 'You want to spend your life digging up old bones and bits of pottery?'

'Hey, big kid, you played with cars for years,' he retorted, laughing.

Alim chuckled. 'Well, if you put it that way...okay, I'm growing up and you're getting to go make mud pies.'

The laughter relaxed them both. 'So you have no objections?'

'I have no right to object to anything you want to do, even if I have the power.' Alim came around the desk, and gave Harun a cocky grin. 'I promise to get the job right, and not bother you or force you home for at least the next thirteen years.'

Harun looked up, his expression hardening. 'Thanks, but I'm not applying for digs just yet. I have something I need to do first.'

Alim tilted his head.

'You just said you wouldn't object to anything I wanted.' Harun shook off Alim's hands as they landed on his shoulders, and stood. 'First, I have to renounce my position formally, publicly state I don't want the job.' He met his brother's eyes. 'I have to disappear until everyone in the nation accepts you in the position, or our friends will try again…and this time they might get it right.'

'I guess I'd better let you do it…but you're all I have left, Harun.' Alim's face seemed to take on a few more lines, or maybe the scars were more pronounced. 'Take care with your life, little *akh*. Don't leave me alone to grieve at your funeral.'

The words were raw, but still Alim squared up to him, looking him in the eye. And Harun realised he was the taller brother—something he'd never noticed before. 'I'm doing this *for* you. I'm the soldier in the family. I have to hunt them down.' He spoke through a throat hurting with unspoken emotion. 'Until the group's disabled, you'll never be safe—and neither will the woman you love.'

'And if I don't want you to do this? If I say that without you, I have nothing?'

Too late, he heard the choked emotion, and understood what Alim wasn't saying. 'What about Hana?'

His brother's jaw hardened still more. 'That's no more open to discussion than your private life with Amber. But let me say this now, while I can, because I know you're going to disappear, no matter what I say. Are you leaving because you hate me for Fadi's death— or can I hope one day you'll forgive me?'

The words sliced Harun when he'd least expected it.

He wheeled away, just trying to breathe for a minute, but his chest felt constricted.

'I have to know, Harun.' The hand that landed on his shoulder was shaking. 'Despite the fact that you were his favourite, I loved him. He was more father than brother to us both from the time we were little.'

All he could do was nod once.

After a stretch of quiet, Alim asked, 'Do you blame me for his death?'

'Stop,' he croaked, feeling as if Alim had torn him in half.

'I need to know, Harun.'

There were so many replies he could make to that assertion, but he'd been where Alim was now. He knew better than Alim did that staffers and servants and all the personal and national wealth that oil and gas could bring, even the adoration of a nation, the whole world, didn't halt the simple loneliness of not having the woman you wanted love you for who you really were inside.

It seemed this was a week of unburdening, whether he wanted to or not.

'Fadi made his own decision,' he said eventually, staring out of the window. 'I always knew that. He was so unhappy at the political marriage he had to make— not just with Amber, but any suitable woman. He loved Rafa with all his heart. I don't think he wanted to die, just to escape from inevitability for a few days.'

After a long time, Alim answered, sounding constricted. 'Thank you.'

He shrugged again. 'You saw how unhappy he was, didn't you? I saw it too, but I didn't know what to do; I had nothing to offer him. You gave him escape for a little while, because you loved him. His death was a terrible accident, one that scars you more than me. I never blamed you for it.' *Only for running off when I needed someone the most,* he thought but didn't say. Alim had more burdens on his shoulders than he'd ever dreamed. He found himself hoping Hana would come back to him, and make him happy.

'Thanks, *akh.*'

Two words straight from the heart, the word *brother* filled with choked emotion, bringing them both a measure of healing—and yet Harun wondered when it was that he'd last heard someone speak to him that way. Fadi had never been one for pretty words, just a clasp on the shoulder in thanks for a job well done.

Do you think...we could maybe go on a honeymoon? Just us, you and me?

Amber had spoken to him from the heart, probably as much as she'd dared when he'd never once told her what he wanted with her—and he realised what he'd done by making his decision without involving her.

He turned back to Alim. 'I need to find Amber.'

Alim nodded. 'That you do, brother. I think it's time—or way past time, actually—that you told her how you feel about her.' Startled, Harun stared at him, and Alim gave a small smile. 'I saw it on your face the day you first saw her, and even in the way you looked at her today. I knew then, but I understand it now. It's how I felt when I first saw Hana. It's how I still feel even though she's gone.'

'You...knew how I felt about Amber?' he asked slowly, taken aback by his brother's insight. Alim saw more about him than he'd ever realised.

Alim shrugged. 'Why do you think I left so quickly after meeting her? I saw the way she looked at me—but the crush was on the Racing Sheikh.'

'So you knew that, too,' he jerked out.

Alim nodded. 'Of course I knew. Do you really think I'd have left you with all this responsibility three years ago if I didn't think you were going to be rewarded with your heart's desire? Leaving without a word to either of you would make her turn to you, because you were as hurt as she was by my disappearance.' By now they were both staring hard out the window, looking at the city view as if it held the answers to life's mysteries.

'Why?' Harun asked eventually. 'Didn't you know I'd rather have had you?'

'Not then, I didn't. I do now.' From the corner of his eye, he saw Alim shrug. 'I was the wrong man for her. I knew you'd step up, take the marriage and position I couldn't bear to. It was selfish, yes, and I wanted to run; but I couldn't stand the thought of taking someone so precious from you—again.'

Fadi. Oh, the guilt Alim carried on his shoulders…

Beyond an answer, Harun shook his head. Unable to stand any more emotion, he joked mildly, 'You always did have the gift of the gab. The only one of us who did.'

'It hasn't got me very far with Hana,' Alim muttered.

Harun resisted the urge to touch his brother's shoulder, and asked again, brother to brother. 'She won't marry you?'

This time Alim shook his head. 'She's running from all the stories. She thinks she isn't worthy to be my wife. I hoped when I met the family that they'd know her worth, but they agreed with her. Her father all but told me to forget her. I can't do that, I'll never do that! As if bloodlines matter when we're all descendants of the one man!'

Harun shrugged. 'There's a world of practical difference between the theory of being a fellow descendant of Abraham, and the reality of being royalty or a miner's daughter.'

'Not to me,' Alim growled. 'Would your ice princess have risked her life to save you—not once, but a half-dozen times?'

'I was only saying what she might be thinking,' Harun replied mildly. He knew when a man spoke from love and pain, and the foolishness of words regretted later, but unable to take back. 'I agree with you. Hana's a heroine, and she has a courage far more suited to the role you want her to take than any pampered princess— but it's what she thinks that counts.'

Mollified, Alim nodded. 'Sorry I jumped on you.'

'Forgiven—but I'd appreciate it if you'd never call Amber an ice princess again,' he added, gently frigid. 'She might not have saved any lives, but she's put up with quite a lot from the el-Kanar brothers, mostly without complaint, and with the kind of loyalty not one of us have earned from her. She forgave you not half an hour ago without even telling you about the very public embarrassment she suffered when you disappeared rather than marry her.'

Alim sobered once more. 'You're right. I apologise— and I think it's time you did, too. Go,' he said, half forceful, half laughing as Harun turned on his heel to stalk down his quarry.

It took him over an hour to find her—and in a night of surprises, she was sitting at a desk in the extensive library, her nose buried in a book on the archaeology of the Near East local area. She glanced up at his approach, but, with a flash of defiance in her eyes, she lowered her gaze to her book, and kept reading.

Fervently wishing for Alim's gift of the gab about

now, his ability to turn a phrase into something emotional and beautiful, Harun could only find his own words. 'I'm sorry. I know you were only trying to help.'

With careful precision, she turned a page, as if she was absorbed by the book. 'What is your plan?'

He didn't hesitate. 'I'm leaving tonight. I have a few leads—I have to find out who abducted us and why. Alim and the entire royal household cannot be safe until they have been brought to justice.'

Her gaze drifted a little further down the page. 'Goodbye, then. Enjoy your escape.'

'Amber, please understand. I have to do this.'

'And of course I'm far safer here, left alone in the place where I was kidnapped last time,' she remarked idly, turning another page. 'But then, I don't suppose my fears and wishes come into this. You're going, and leaving me here, no matter how I feel about it.'

The observation jolted him. 'I thought you of all people would understand. You said there wasn't anything you wouldn't do to save your family.'

'Hmm? What was that?' She ran her finger down a page before she looked up with a cloudy-eyed expression.

'Don't be childish,' he rebuked in an undertone.

Her brows lifted in a look of mild surprise. 'Sorry, I can hardly believe you're still here talking to me. You should be off saving your brother, your nation or anything else. After all, isn't he all you have? Isn't your duty to your brother and country above everything, especially me?'

That hit hard. 'I have to do this, Amber. If I don't disappear and hunt them down, they'll just take us again— or kill Alim to make me step up, now they know we're lovers.'

'We were lovers,' she replied, still in that indolent, I-don't-care voice. 'Rather hard to be anything when you're going undercover commando on me.'

Right now he wished she'd just say what she wanted, but she'd gone Ice Queen on him again, and it was taking all he had left after this long, very hard day not to respond in kind, or just walk away. 'When I'm done with this, I'm coming back for you.' He tried to smile. 'I want that honeymoon we agreed on.'

At that, she closed the book with a tiny snapping sound. 'Again, it's rather hard to believe that there will be a future at all when you're going to be outnumbered and if they find you, they'll probably kill you—' With a choking sound, she jumped up, wheeled around and ran from the room.

But not before he'd heard her gasp for breath on a sob, and seen her dash the tears from her eyes—and when he tried to find her, to make things right somehow, she'd retired to the section of the palace reserved only for women, where even Alim could not enter.

CHAPTER THIRTEEN

Four months later

'I UNEQUIVOCALLY *refuse any position that belongs right-fully to my brother. I was never more than his care-taker while he healed. I have now handed over the full power to my brother Alim. I am leaving Abbas al-Din tonight, and will not be returning for a long time. I wish my beloved brother happiness in the life ordained for him by God, and fully approve of his choice of bride. Hana al-Sud is a fine, strong woman of faith, worthy of the highest position. Thank you and good evening.'*

For the five hundredth time Amber felt the potent cocktail of hunger and fury as she watched the re-run of the security closed circuit TV. Harun stepped down from the podium at the ruling congress, refusing to an-swer any questions after reading his statement. A five-minute presentation before the people he suspected of abducting them, and then he'd disappeared. No one had heard from him since.

At least, she hadn't. She assumed Alim would tell her something if he knew, but he was very busy, taking the reins of power, planning his wedding—and since com-ing to the palace to accept Alim's proposal, Hana had a terrible habit of dragging him into secret corners to kiss and touch him whenever he had a minute to himself.

Why didn't I think of doing that with Harun years ago?

Because Hana's secure; she knows Alim loves her. She's a blessed woman.

With an angry snap she switched off the TV, resolving for the five hundredth time to never watch again, but she knew she would. Again before bed tonight, leaving her to pace the floor until exhaustion drove her to bed; again tomorrow when she'd finished the studies she loved, but he did too—and before dinner, driving her to eat next to nothing as she uttered polite inanities with the family to prove to them that she was coping with her isolated life, studying an archaeology course in half the time, and living in the old women's quarters with only one maid and guard for company.

Hana and Alim's wedding was to take place in two days. She didn't even assume Harun would return for that event. She'd made that mistake for their engagement party, dressing in her finest, making sure she looked her best...and it was all for nothing.

Alim had no best man. He said if Harun didn't come he didn't want anyone.

She knew exactly how Alim felt. Why, why couldn't she just leave him behind, as he'd done with her? Why didn't she just get on with her life?

'Because I have nowhere to go,' she muttered, leaping to her feet and crossing the room rather than give in to the temptation to throw something at the TV. Despite her station, she had no personal fortune, or even a bank account. Not one of the staff in the palace, even a foreign worker, would help her, at the risk of deportation; her face was too well known. Her father refused to allow her to stay with them, or even send the jet for a week's visit.

Come when your husband returns to claim you, he'd said inflexibly.

And unless it was to family, the law of the land forbade her from leaving her husband unless she could prove ongoing physical abuse. She had no friends outside her family circle, nobody close that would offer her shelter, or believe her if she tried to claim abuse; they'd all loved Harun from the start.

No, she was a royal wife in a traditional land: just another possession left unwanted in the treasure room until her owner remembered her.

Instead of pacing the floor for the five hundredth time, she stared fiercely out of the window. What she wouldn't give to grow wings right now! She'd escaped once, but this time she was surrounded less by snipers than a thousand servants catering to her every need, and watching her every move. They were her protectors until her husband came back to take over the job. So until Harun chose to return from his wanderings and release her, she was caged as effectively as she'd been for her abductors.

Two days later

'So, *akh,* I hear you're one best man short.'

With an hour until the wedding Alim, standing alone in the sheikh's magnificent bedchamber and dressed in his groom's finery, whirled around to see Harun in the doorway, with a cheeky grin. Tired to the point of falling down, he was still ready to give his brother support during his day of days.

He threw Alim a mock salute. 'Your Highness.'

And found himself smothered in a hard embrace. '*Akh,* little *akh,* praise God you're alive.' Alim was trembling. 'I thought…feared…'

'I can hardly breathe here,' he complained with a laugh. 'I'm okay, *akh,* really—and when you come back from your honeymoon, I have good news to report.'

Alim pulled back, but hugged him again. 'I'll be grateful for that later. Right now, my little brother's back from the dead… It was so damn *hard* going through my transition and engagement alone. I wanted you with me, to share my happiness and hardships.'

Harun willed away the sense of irony in everything Alim had just said. Telling Alim he'd felt the same for years would only damage their fragile relationship; he understood, and that was enough. 'If it helps, I worked day and night the past few months to get here today.'

Alim peered at his face, and frowned. 'You do look like you're ready to fall down. Come, take some coffee. I can't have you falling asleep on me during the ceremony.' Alim led him inside, and poured him a cup of thick, syrupy black coffee. 'There's more. I've been drinking it all day.'

Harun chuckled and shook his head. 'No wonder you seem like one of those wind-up toys. Why are you so nervous? You know Hana loves you.'

Alim sobered. 'You know her first marriage was a sham. It's her first time tonight, as well as our first time. If I don't—'

Harun silenced him with a lifted hand, smiling. 'I was there a few months ago, *akh.* Take it from one who knows now. I've seen the way she looks at you in news reports, and heard how she drags you into cupboards.' Alim chuckled at that, as Harun intended. 'She loves you, Alim; she's ready. It will be everything she's dreamed of, because in her eyes, that's what you are.'

'That was—the perfect thing to say.' He was taken aback by Alim's hand cupping his cheek. 'I can't believe you came back for me.'

So much left unsaid, but it no longer needed to be said. 'Ah, you know me. I'm always hanging around just waiting to be useful.'

Alim grabbed the coffee cup from him and drew him into the stranglehold hug again, thumping him on the back. 'I don't deserve you, but I thank Allah every day for the gifts you've given me.'

'You found life's best gift all by yourself. You came home all by yourself, too. I had my bride and my life handed to me—by you, I should add.'

'You know what I mean. I can't believe we could have been friends all these years, but—'

Neither wanted to say it. Separated by those they'd loved and needed most, they could always have been allies. 'Nothing's stopping us now,' Harun said huskily.

'And nothing will again.' Another massive hug.

'You're choking me,' Harun mock complained, 'and crushing my best man's outfit.'

'Who was it that abducted you?' Alim asked abruptly, releasing him.

In answer, he handed Alim the file he'd dropped during the first hug. 'The entire group has been put out of action.'

'Hmm.' Alim scanned the first sheet rapidly. 'I wouldn't have thought it of the Jamal and Hamor clans, but yes, they are very conservative. With financial and armed backing from our more conservative neighbours, I guess they thought they could try. I think it's time we did something about our neighbours, too.'

'I did all that's needed, My Lord.' Harun bowed, laughing again. 'I told you I worked night and day. I found out who it was by word of mouth months ago—but proof had to be absolute. When it was, the perpetrators were easy to rout, especially after my public announcement. Now go, enjoy your wedding. It's time to go see your bride.'

And he pushed Alim out of the door. One relationship on track…but he had the feeling this lifelong breach would be the easier of the two to heal.

The wedding banquet was beautiful, filled with the daintiest dishes of the region. Sheikhs, presidents and first ladies sat at the tables, mingled and laughed, probably proposed or made new deals over a relaxing extended meal, while Alim and Hana ignored the world, feeding each other, giving small touches, their eyes locked on the other. So absorbed were they that when someone approached them, they jerked out of their own little world with obvious surprise that anyone else existed.

To think he could have had a similar wedding, if only he'd known Amber wanted him the way he'd wanted her…

But right now, even his memories of their two days of joy seemed false. Dressed in full, traditional clothing, covered from head to foot apart from her face, Amber sat at the royal table between two first ladies, speaking only with them. She was thinner, paler, wearing none of her soft make-up that made her face glow with life; her eyes were too calm, holding no emotion at all; her hands remained at the table instead of waving around as she talked.

She'd lost herself somewhere in the past few

months—or hours. She'd whitened when she'd seen him standing beside Alim, and looked away before he could move or even smile at her, and she'd avoided him ever since. He'd been trying to get her attention discreetly, but she wasn't responding. Any moment now, she'd excuse herself and retire to the women's quarters.

So he stalked over to her. 'I wish to speak to you, my wife.'

Amber's head snapped around to him, her lips parted in shock that he'd come right into the open; but trapped by law and convention, she could either cause a scene, or acquiesce.

The cheeks that had been pale were now rosy; her eyes were fiery with indignation. 'As you can no doubt see, I am fully occupied at present, my husband.' With the slightest sarcastic inflection on the title *husband,* she waved a hand at the important women sitting either side of her, who both immediately demurred, insisting that if her husband wished to speak with her, they'd be fine together.

Obviously fuming, she rose to her feet; but Harun, inwardly grinning—at least she was alive again—held out his hand, which again she had to take in seeming grace. He led her around the table, and out through the state banqueting rooms onto the back balcony of the palace, semi-private and with no public or press access.

Once there, she jerked her hand away, and folded her arms, waiting.

Instinct told him a joke wouldn't get him far this time. Neither would she reach out to him. This time, he had to be the one to give. Anything that would get her to talk to him, tell him what she was thinking and feeling, even if she hated him.

So he started there. 'Do you hate me for being away so long?'

She sighed, looking out into the night. 'Why don't you tell me what you want from me this time, so we can get on with our lives once you're gone again?'

The question confused him, but he felt it wasn't a topic to pursue, not yet. 'You look so thin,' he said softly. 'Are you feeling well?'

'I'm fine, thank you.' Cold words, with no compromise. She wasn't giving anything away, wasn't going to play his game. She wanted her question answered.

'You're my wife. I've come back for you, as I promised I would.'

'Like a dropped-off package, or a toy forgotten about until you want to play again?'

'No, like a wife I hoped would understand that what I was doing had to come first.'

Another sigh, harsh and rather bored, and she kept looking out into the night. 'Just tell me what you want.'

He shook his head. 'I don't understand. You're my wife. I've come back for you.'

'Your wife.' The words were flat, as was the laughter that followed. 'So says the imam that performed the service. Isn't that what you said?' Still she wouldn't look at him. 'What is a wife to you?'

She'd obviously had far too much time alone to think; every question she asked left him feeling more bewildered. 'I think you have ideas on what I think a wife is.' Soft, provocatively spoken, designed to break the wall of ice around her and get to the pain of abandonment hiding beneath.

She lifted her brows in open incredulity, but remained silent.

Feeling hunted and harried into a position he didn't

want to take, wishing fervently for the wife who'd pushed and prodded her way into his bed and heart, he snapped, 'Okay, Amber, I don't know what I think a wife is, but I know what I want. I want those two days we had. I want them again. I want a honeymoon with you, to find the life we both want—'

Loud, almost manic laughter sliced his words off. Amber was doubled over herself, laughing with a hard, cynical edge that told him he'd better not join her. 'A life we both want?' She gasped, and laughed over again. 'What do *I* want, Harun? Do you even know that much about me? Do you know anything about me?'

Daylight began cracking apart the icy darkness she'd wrapped herself in. 'I know you're brave and beautiful and loyal to me even when I don't deserve it,' he said softly. 'I know you gave me chance after chance, and forgave me time and again. I know you're the wife I want, the woman I want to spend my life with. But you're right, I don't know what you want. That's what I'm here to find out. Doesn't that count for something?'

'Not right now, no.' Hands on hips, she seemed challenging, except she still refused to look at him, or make a connection of any kind. If she'd heard how he felt about her written between the lines he'd spoken she wouldn't acknowledge it.

'All right, Amber, I understand.'

A little snort was her only answer.

'Oh, I do understand.' With swift, military precision, he whipped the burqa from her head, ignoring her outraged gasp. 'You're hiding from me the way I hid from you all those years. You're not going to make it easy for me, and I don't deserve you to.' Grabbing her and hauling her against him, he held her hard with one hand, while he slowly played with a thick tress of hair, unbound beneath the veil she'd worn. 'Have I missed anything?' he asked huskily, inhaling the rose-mary scent in her hair.

'Ask yourself,' she retorted in a voice that shook just a little.

'Ah, thank you, *mee johara*. That means I did.' He grinned at her as her eyes smoked with fury. 'Ah, of course…you still want to know what I think a wife is?'

Her chin lifted.

'You,' he answered, trying to douse the flames in her heart. 'That's all. When I think of "a wife", I think of you. Just as you are.'

'Don't,' she snarled without warning. 'Don't worm your way in with pretty words and compliments. I thought you were dead—that—that they'd killed you. Or that you were never coming back. Why else would you not contact me once? What did I do to—to…?' She pulled at his hands until he released her. She'd startled him right out of his cocky assurance, and his belief that he'd win. She faced him, panting, her eyes shimmer-ing with pain. 'I *loved* you. I loved you with all of me, I gave you everything I had, and you just left. You left me for the sake of the brother who'd abandoned and be-trayed you. Do you have any idea what that did to me?'

Bewildered, he spoke from depths he hadn't known were in him. 'But he's my family, Amber. I had no choice. It was my duty.'

'What about me?' she cried. 'Was it your *duty* to se-duce and then abandon me, to hurt me the way Alim hurt you? Do I have to run off like he did to make you see I'm alive and that I *hurt?*' She held up a hand when he would have spoken. 'I—I can't do this any more. I tried, Harun, I tried to make things work with you for three years. I tried to show you that love isn't manipulation and emotional blackmail, but you won't see it. I'm tired of hitting my head against a wall. Believe Fadi and not me, and spend your life alone!'

She ran for the balcony doors.

Love isn't manipulation and emotional blackmail... believe Fadi...

That was what Fadi had done to him since childhood, and he'd never known it until now. But she had. She'd seen that he'd gained Fadi's love and approval by doing anything asked of him, no matter what it cost him personally. Fadi hadn't known any better, but followed the example set by their parents. Alim had found a way to escape from it, and somehow, somewhere in his worldwide travels, had learned how to love. But he, Harun, had stayed like a whipped dog, always saying yes, because he accepted the manipulation—because he didn't know any better.

In three long years, Amber had asked only one thing of him—and he hadn't even given her that, because she didn't manipulate or blackmail him into it.

*If someone loves you, they ask the impossible over and over...*and he'd believed it was normal, even right; his duty.

Amber hadn't asked him to change, or to slay dragons for her. So he'd never believed she loved him. Not until now, when she'd stripped his lifelong beliefs in a moment, left him bare and bleeding, and she was leaving him.

He couldn't stand it, couldn't take losing her. This time would be for ever—

'I love you.' Three raw, desperate words. *God, let them be enough, let her stay. Come back to me, Amber...*

Her hand on the door handle, she turned, and hope soared—

She made a small, choking sound, the one she made when she was about to cry. 'I can't believe you'd be so cruel, after what they did to you. Don't ever use those words against me again.'

Then she was gone. Harun stood by the balcony rail, exposed to the bone, the world's greatest fool.

CHAPTER FOURTEEN

It was 3 a.m. and Harun was pounding the road, gasping with each breath and pushing himself still harder. At least ten miles from the palace, his guards were running behind him and finding it hard to keep up. It had been hours since he'd seen Alim and Hana to their bridal chamber. He'd shepherded all of the guests downstairs, made sure the food and drink still overflowed for anyone who wanted it. He'd chatted amiably with heads of state he'd known for years, had quietly warned their friendlier neighbours against trusting certain people among the nations surrounding them, and in general played the perfect host.

The perfect host, the perfect brother, he thought now, with an inner wryness that never made it to his expression. *Why can't I be the perfect husband?*

He wished he knew how to be everything Amber wanted…

What does she want? an imp in his mind prodded. *All she ever wanted was you. But you pushed her away and abandoned her until it was too late. What does she want now—the freedom from you she'd asked for months ago?*

Her words replayed over and over in his brain. *I*

thought you were dead. Or that you were never coming back. Love isn't manipulation and emotional blackmail.

He was missing something. It wasn't in Amber's nature to hurt him without a reason; he knew that now. Everything she'd said taught him what love wasn't.

So what the hell *was* it, then? It seemed she had the secret, but he'd been deaf and blind the whole time she was trying to tell or show him.

He thought she'd *wanted* to hear he loved her. So what had gone so wrong?

At four a.m., he came to the inescapable conclusion: there was only one way to find out. He wheeled around and ran back for the palace, much to the relief of his stitching, gasping guards.

Five a.m.

'My Lord, it's written in the law! You cannot come into this place!'

'Unless you are the ruling sheikh—or the woman in question is your wife. I know the law. Is there any woman in here but my wife?'

'There is the maid, My Lord!'

'Then I suggest you send her out immediately. I will give you three minutes, then I am coming in no matter what—and I suggest you don't argue with me. I doubt you possess the skills to stop me.'

'Your wife is sleeping. Would you wake her?'

'No, she's not. She's behind the door, listening, as she has been since about a minute after I began yelling for her. I knew she'd be awake, or I wouldn't have come.'

The tone was more grim than amused. Even with her throat and eyes on fire, Amber smiled a bit. The door had no glass; he'd just known she'd be waiting for him.

'Let him in, Tahir,' she called, opening the door. 'I'll send Sabetha out.'

The maid, wakened by Harun's first roar for Amber, scuttled past her. Harun shouldered past the guard, snarling, 'No listening. If there's any gossip about this, you both lose your positions.'

'We love the lady Amber, My Lord,' little, delicate Sabetha said, with gentle dignity.

His face softened at that. 'I'm grateful for your loyalty to the lady Amber. I beg your pardon for insulting you.'

Sabetha smiled up at him, not with infatuation but instant affection. Tahir smiled also, but with a manly kind of understanding; he'd forgiven his lord.

Harun seemed to have the knack of making people care. She just wished he knew how to care in return.

In softer mode now, he walked into the room and closed the door. But instead of talking, he just looked at her until she wanted to squirm. 'Well?' she demanded, or tried to. It sounded breathless, hopeful.

Would she ever stop being a fool over this man?

'You are the most beautiful thing I've ever seen or will ever see,' he said, with a quiet sincerity that made her breath take up unmoving lodgings in her throat. 'I thought that the first time I saw you, and I still think it now.'

She lifted her chin, letting him see her devastated face clearly, her tangled hair and the salt tracks lining her cheeks. 'I've spent the past six hours crying and hating you, so it might be best if you use less practised lines. You have five minutes to give me a compelling reason to let you stay here any longer.'

'That you've cried over me only makes you more beautiful in my eyes.'

'That's nice.' Tapping her foot, she looked at her watch. 'Four minutes forty-five seconds.'

He closed his eyes. 'I don't know how to love any other way but through doing what I perceived as my duty. I thought it was all I had to give.' Taking her by the shoulders, he opened his eyes, looked at her as if she was his path to salvation and rushed the words out, as if he didn't say everything now, he never would. 'Those two days we were together, I felt like I was fly- ing. Now it's gone, and the past few months I felt like I was starving to death. I'm suffocating under duty, lost and wandering and alone, and nothing works. I need you, Amber, by God I need you. Please, can you teach me how to make you happy—because without you, I never will be. I can't sleep, I can't eat, can't think about anything but touching you, being with you again.' He dragged her against him, and she didn't have the heart or will to pull away. 'Don't deny me, Amber, because I won't go, not tonight, not any night. Teach me the words you want to hear. I'll say whatever you need, do whatever it takes, because right now I need you more than my next breath. I can't let you keep shutting me out, not when you're everything to me.'

Ouch—it hurt to try to gulp with her mouth still open. How did he turn up just when she'd given up hope, and say the words she needed to hear more than life?

With a tiny noise, she buried her face in his neck. 'Me too, oh, me too, I need you so much,' she whispered as she cannoned into him, her fingers winding in his hair to pull him down to her. 'You just said everything I needed to know.'

'Except one thing,' he muttered hoarsely between kisses. 'I love you, Amber. I have from the day we met.

I just never knew how to say it, or how to believe you could ever love me in return.'

'Do you believe it now?' she whispered, pulling back a little. This was something she had to know now.

He smiled down at her. 'I knew it the day you yelled at Alim, my jewel. It's why I came back today so full of confidence. I'd hoped missing me would have softened you. But you taught me a valuable lesson tonight—that I have to trust in our love, and talk to you.' He nuzzled her lips. 'I'll never put you last again. From now on, you're my family, my first duty. My desire, my passion. My precious jewel.'

'I'm so happy,' she cried, kissing him. 'But though your words are wonderful, I want you to show me the desire and passion. I've missed you so much!'

He didn't need to be told twice. Devouring each other in desperate kisses, mumbling more words of desire and need, they staggered together back to the bed.

Later that morning

The sun was well up when Harun began to stir.

Amber was curled against him like a contented cat, her head on his chest, her body wound around his, one leg and arm holding him to her. He smiled, and kissed the top of her head. Her hair was splayed across his body; her breaths warmed his skin.

Unable to make the mat to give his morning prayer, he gave his thanks in silence, deep and heartfelt. *Thank you for helping me find the way back to her again.*

They'd made love twice, first in a frenzy and then slow and ecstatic. They'd said words of need and pleasure and love during the past four hours.

Now it was time for the next step.

'Amber.' He bent his head to kiss the top of her head. 'Love, we need to talk. No, I said *talk*, my jewel.' He laughed as she kissed his chest, slow and sensuous. 'I've made some arrangements for us I hope you'll like.'

'Mmm-hmm,' she mumbled through kisses. 'Tell me.'

'Are you listening?' He laughed again. She was peppering his torso with kisses and caresses, and he was getting distracted.

'Uh-huh, I always listen to you. Mmm…' More kisses. 'Hurry, *habibi*, it's been at least two hours since we made love. I need you.'

'I've secured us two part-time, unpaid places on a dig only half an hour's drive from the University of Araba Numara…and while I do my doctorate, you'll be finishing your course face to face.'

That stopped her. Completely. She gaped up at him. 'You know about my course?'

'Why do you think I applied for positions near that university? I've known everything you've been doing the past four months—and it made me so proud of you.'

'You—you don't mind?' she asked, half shyly. 'About being a woman and getting all high distinctions, I mean?'

'No, of course not—I've heard you've got lots of distinctions—I'm so proud of you. I've never felt threatened by your intelligence, Amber,' he said quietly. 'And I trust you completely. As I said, your success has made me so proud of you, *mee johara*. I married a woman of great intellect as well as good taste—in loving history and her husband.' He winked at her. 'Do my arrangements meet with your approval?'

'Approval? Oh, you have no idea! I love you, I love you!'

'We'll be living in the same tents as everyone else,

I warn you,' he put in with mock-sternness, but was turning to fire again at her touch. 'And it will mean no babies until you're done with your course.'

Again she looked up at him, almost in wonder. 'You don't mind waiting for children?'

'I've waited all this time for you,' he murmured, with the utmost tenderness. 'I can wait a little more for our family to start.'

'I love you,' she whispered again, with all the vivid intensity of her nature, and pulled him down on top of her.

Strange how falling down actually felt like flying...

EPILOGUE

Eight years later

'It's a girl!'

In the sorting tent, deep in diagnosis of the siftings he'd just dug up, Harun frowned vaguely at his wife's excited voice coming from behind him. 'Hmm? What was that?'

'Harun, we have a new niece. Hana had a girl about an hour ago.'

'That's great. Look at this piece I found, *mee johara*. Is this beer jug belly Sumerian, do you think?'

'Harun, look at me.' Gently he was turned around. He knew, having finished her archaeology degree last year, as excited by the past as he could ever hope for, Amber wouldn't risk disturbing his findings. But, as she always said, *without families there wouldn't be history to discover.* 'Hana had a girl an hour ago. They named her Johara.'

The look in Amber's eyes warned him to return to the present. He blinked, focusing on what he'd only half-heard, and slowly grinned. 'That's wonderful! We have a niece at last. Kalila will be thrilled.'

Their five-year-old daughter always felt left out of her boy cousins' rowdy play. She was a girly-girl, and even though she was as enthusiastic as her parents on the digs, she somehow managed to stay clean. The only time she had someone as fastidious as her on the digs was when Naima stayed for the school breaks. Kalila adored her cousin, and followed her around like a puppy.

At not yet four, their son Tarif fitted in splendidly with his male cousins, rolling around as happily on the palace floors, indulging in masculine play with his father and uncle. But when on the dig, he confined his rougher antics to the hours Harun kept sacred for play with his son. He knew better than to disturb any promising-looking holes in the ground, though Harun swore their son was a genius from the day he'd inadvertently found the site of an ancient temple's foundations when he was trying to poke in a snake hole. 'Abi, Abi, pretty rocks over there,' he'd said, growing distressed until Harun followed his little son to the other side of the *tell,* where they hadn't yet sectioned off the ground to look.

Amber grinned. 'I've booked the jet for Monday. I can't fly after that, as you know—' the slight stress on *know* told him if he didn't remember she was twenty-seven weeks pregnant, he'd better catch up with real life and fast '—and I want to see my…well, my sort-of namesake.'

'Oh, of course she is.' Harun grinned again. 'I'm sure they named her for you, my jewel,' he assured her with mock-gravity.

Laughing, she swatted him with her fingers. 'You could at least pretend to believe it. You know I'm in a very delicate state right now.'

Both brows lifted with that one. 'Um, yes, very delicate,' he agreed. 'Remind me again how your delicate condition meant you had to crawl ahead of me five days ago into an unstable subterranean chamber?' Not to mention that, at night, she was the one to instigate loving as often as he did. They'd have at least six children by now, if they hadn't planned their family carefully around Amber's studies.

Finding no answer for his teasing, Amber put her nose in the air; then she looked at the small piece he'd found. 'Oh, I do concur, it is part of a beer jug, and it definitely looks the right period. It's a shame it isn't Amalekite. We're still not there,' she teased, backing off as he mock waved his fist at her. 'It's a very good piece. But you might want to call the family and congratulate them before you get lost in the Sumerian period again,' she suggested, turning his face back to her as her opinion distracted him. 'One more,' she murmured, kissing him again, deepening it to keep him in the here and now.

'One more kiss like that and I'll forget the Sumerian artefact as well as our new niece,' he mock threatened as his body awoke.

'Not you, my love,' she retorted, laughing. 'And anyway, there's always tonight.'

As if on cue, the baby kicked its father, squirming around as if to say, *Not again, you two!* It was a chant almost everyone on any dig said to them, sooner or later. Whether it was over their almost scary connection over their love of ancient history or their knowledge of ancient finds, or their touching and kissing so often when they were together, the protest was as loud as it was meant in fun. *I wish I could find what you two have,* was the lament of so many people on the digs, when another relationship failed with someone who could never understand the archaeologist's absorbing passion for the past.

'Okay, little one, okay,' he said softly, caressing Amber's

belly, leaning down to kiss his child. 'I think you're being told to rest, my jewel.'

'I think I am.' She smothered a yawn. 'Tarif will wake in about an hour, so I'd better get there.' She gave him one final kiss. 'But I want to hear all about the jug later—and don't think the other part of tonight's forgotten, either.'

'Never,' he assured her with a wink. 'Both have been duly noted.'

'And call Alim,' she reminded him a final time, at the tent flap. 'Don't forget to call Naima too. Tell her the car will pick her up the day we arrive, if Buhjah doesn't have anything else planned for her.'

Grinning, he waved in acceptance. Amber returned to their family tent where Tarif still slept in a partitioned-off section, and at the other end Kalila endured her long-suffering tutor's lessons on mathematics.

Harun, smiling as he always did when Amber had been with him or when he thought of his family, pulled out his phone to call his niece. Naima was thrilled she had a new girl cousin, and, after consulting with Buhjah, told him she could join in the family celebrations. He chatted with her for a few minutes longer, hearing all about her studies and her other family, the antics of her younger half-brothers at home, before hanging up with a smile.

Then he called the palace to congratulate Alim and Hana, and to hear about his new niece. The bubbling joy in his brother's voice when he spoke of their new 'little jewel' made Harun's cup run over.

He was a blessed man.

* * * * *

COMING NEXT MONTH from Harlequin® Romance
AVAILABLE JULY 2, 2012

#4321 THE RANCHER'S HOUSEKEEPER
In Her Shoes...
Rebecca Winters
Rugged rancher Colt Brannigan hires mysterious
Geena Williams as his housekeeper. But is this beautiful
stranger trouble with a capital *T?*

#4322 THE COWBOY COMES HOME
The Larkville Legacy
Patricia Thayer
Single mom Jess Calhoun catches the eye of cowboy
Johnny Jameson. Can this wild wanderer settle down in
sleepy Larkville?

#4323 BATTLE FOR THE SOLDIER'S HEART
Cara Colter
Cynical Rory is drawn to Grace's sweetness. But she
mustn't fall for him—he's all kinds of wrong for her....

#4324 THE LAST WOMAN HE'D EVER DATE
Liz Fielding
Journalist Claire Thackeray wants the inside scoop
on the new owner of Cranbrook Park—her teen crush,
brooding Hal North!

#4325 ONE DAY TO FIND A HUSBAND
The McKenna Brothers
Shirley Jump
Ellie's wish to adopt baby Jiao hits a husband-size
hump! So she proposes a merger-with-a-twist with
business rival Finn McKenna....

#4326 INVITATION TO THE PRINCE'S PALACE
Jennie Adams
Mel's just a normal girl until a cab ride with
Prince Rikardo becomes an invitation to a whole
new life!

HRCNM0612

REQUEST YOUR FREE BOOKS!
2 FREE NOVELS PLUS 2 FREE GIFTS!

❧ Harlequin®

Romance

From the Heart, For the Heart

YES! Please send me 2 FREE Harlequin® Romance novels and my 2 FREE gifts (gifts are worth about $10). After receiving them, if I don't wish to receive any more books, I can return the shipping statement marked "cancel". If I don't cancel, I will receive 6 brand-new novels every month and be billed just $4.09 per book in the U.S. or $4.49 per book in Canada. That's a savings of at least 14% off the cover price! It's quite a bargain! Shipping and handling is just 50¢ per book in the U.S. and 75¢ per book in Canada.* I understand that accepting the 2 free books and gifts places me under no obligation to buy anything. I can always return a shipment and cancel at any time. Even if I never buy another book, the two free books and gifts are mine to keep forever.

116/316 HDN FESE

Name _____ (PLEASE PRINT)

Address _____ Apt. #

City _____ State/Prov. _____ Zip/Postal Code

Signature (if under 18, a parent or guardian must sign)

Mail to the **Reader Service:**
IN U.S.A.: P.O. Box 1867, Buffalo, NY 14240-1867
IN CANADA: P.O. Box 609, Fort Erie, Ontario L2A 5X3

Not valid for current subscribers to Harlequin Romance books.

**Are you a subscriber to Harlequin Romance books
and want to receive the larger-print edition?
Call 1-800-873-8635 or visit www.ReaderService.com.**

* Terms and prices subject to change without notice. Prices do not include applicable taxes. Sales tax applicable in N.Y. Canadian residents will be charged applicable taxes. Offer not valid in Quebec. This offer is limited to one order per household. All orders subject to credit approval. Credit or debit balances in a customer's account(s) may be offset by any other outstanding balance owed by or to the customer. Please allow 4 to 6 weeks for delivery. Offer available while quantities last.

Your Privacy—The Reader Service is committed to protecting your privacy. Our Privacy Policy is available online at www.ReaderService.com or upon request from the Reader Service.

We make a portion of our mailing list available to reputable third parties that offer products we believe may interest you. If you prefer that we not exchange your name with third parties, or if you wish to clarify or modify your communication preferences, please visit us at www.ReaderService.com/consumerschoice or write to us at Reader Service Preference Service, P.O. Box 9062, Buffalo, NY 14269. Include your complete name and address.

Looking for a great Western read?

Harlequin Books has just the thing!

A Cowboy for Every Mood

Look for the Stetson flash
on all Western titles this summer!

Pick up a cowboy book
by some of your favorite authors:

Vicki Lewis Thompson
B.J. Daniels
Patricia Thayer
Cathy McDavid
And many more...

Available wherever books are sold.

Saddle up with Harlequin® and visit
www.Harlequin.com

*Patricia Thayer welcomes you to Larkville, Texas,
in THE COWBOY COMES HOME—book 1 in the exciting
new 8-book miniseries,* **THE LARKVILLE LEGACY,**
from Harlequin® Romance.

REACHING THE BANK, Jess climbed down, smiling as she walked her mount to the water. "Wow, I haven't ridden like that in years."

"You're good."

"I'm Clay Calhoun's daughter. I'm supposed to be a good rider."

"You miss him."

She walked with him through the stiff winter grass to the tree. "It's hard to imagine the Double Bar C going on without him. He loved this land." She glanced around the landscape. "Now my brother runs the operation, but he'll be gone awhile." She released a breath. "I have to say we miss his leadership."

He frowned. "Is there anything I can do?"

"Thank you. You're handling Storm—that's a big enough help. It's just that it would be nice to have my brothers and sister here." She looked at him. "Do you have any siblings?"

He shook his head. "None that I know of."

"What about your father?" she asked.

He shook his head. "Never been in my life. I tried for years to track him down, but I never could catch up with him."

He caught the sadness etched on her face. "Johnny, I'm sorry."

He hated pity, especially from her. "Why? You had nothing to do with it. Jake Jameson didn't want to be found, or meet his son." He shrugged. "You can't miss what you've never had. I'm not much of a homebody, either. I guess that's why I like to keep moving."

Jess looked out over the land. "I guess that's where we're different. I've never really moved away from Larkville."

"Why should you want to leave? You have your business here and your home."

She smiled. "I had to fight Dad to live on my own. But I've got a little Calhoun stubbornness, too."

"You got all the beauty."

Johnny came closer, removed her hat and studied her face. "Your eyes are incredible. And your mouth... I could kiss you for hours."

She sucked in a breath and raised her gaze to his. "Johnny... We weren't going to start this."

"Don't look now, darlin', but it's already started."

Find out what happens between Johnny and Jess in
THE COWBOY COMES HOME by Patricia Thayer,
available July 2012!

And find out how Jess's family will be transformed
in the 8-book series:
THE LARKVILLE LEGACY
A secret letter...two families changed forever

This summer, celebrate everything Western
with Harlequin® Books!

www.Harlequin.com/Western

HREXP0712